A SINIST
FROM WITHIN...

Arthur Zoran knew something odd was happening on Earth. Two years earlier when Arthur had left for his mission to Cyprian II everything was fine. His first letter from Ardyth had seemed so normal, pouring her heart out about her loneliness over his leaving. But when her next letters arrived heavily censored, Arthur knew something was terribly amiss back on his home planet. And now, two years later, his worst fears were confirmed. Arriving back on Earth he discovered the world was in the throes of a planet-wide invasion. The enemies were called syns—short for "synthetic men." These syns, who were virtually identical to normal human beings, had been infiltrating the human race for some time—and mankind had to stop them before it was too late. But when the love of Arthur's life was fingered as a syn, he knew the facts about the "invasion" weren't as clear-cut as men had been led to believe. So Arthur, against all odds, decided to do something about it…

FOR A COMPLETE SECOND NOVEL, TURN TO PAGE 123

Author Portrait

Raymond F. Jones 1915-1994.

DIVIDED WE FALL

By
RAYMOND F. JONES

ARMCHAIR FICTION
PO Box 4369, Medford, Oregon 97504

The original text of this novel was first published by Ziff-Davis Publishing Company.

For more information about Armchair Books and products, visit our website at...

www.armchairfiction.com

Or email us at...

armchairfiction@yahoo.com

CHAPTER ONE

THE EIGHTEEN-MONTH job on Cyprian II was done and Arthur Zoran was coming home. Counting travel time both ways, he had been away from Earth a full two years.

Through his stateroom window, he watched the disc of Earth, growing as the liner neared home. He imagined the face of Ardyth framed in that circle like a picture in a locket. He could see her as he remembered her, a piquant, inquisitive face with very wide, brown eyes. Her expression was one of perpetual amazement at the wonder of the common things of Earth. Her hair was deep, golden brown, cut short and pressed close to her head in the fashion of the times—which Arthur did not like.

She'd be waiting there at the pier for him; she'd spot him as he left the port and ran down the gangway. She'd wave and call his name in that breathless voice that could send little chills through him. Then she'd be in his arms again, and everything would be as it was before.

Two years.

Six letters.

He sat at the desk and glanced at those letters, which he had laid out there. He didn't need to look at them anymore. He knew them by memory now.

The most recent was six months old—three months to reach him, plus his own three-month journey home. None of the letters were the kind a man expects to receive from the woman he is to marry. Only the first one, which arrived on the next ship after he reached Cyprian II, was full of loss at his leaving and anticipation of the time he would return.

The second and third were heavily censored until scarcely a single intelligible line remained. It was a strange and frightening thing, for there had been no censorship when Arthur left Earth, nor any cause for such.

The men of his work crew were equally puzzled and alarmed by their own communications from home, so heavily garbled by the black swabs, but no one had any answers.

Then these final three letters came through complete as if censoring had been abandoned, but Ardyth spoke then as if Arthur had fully understood the earlier ones.

"The eradication of Syns has gotten fully out of hand," she wrote. "Some of us have begun to wonder if the world will ever be the same again. It can't be for those of us who have seen helpless creatures dragged through the streets and killed by crazed mobs.

"We know the Syns are not human, perhaps not even living things in any sense, but that does not excuse the brutality and terror that has swept the cities. No one feels safe or sure these days. One's most intimate friends might turn out to be Syns, to be dragged away and slaughtered. People hardly speak to one another anymore. Workers go from the laboratories and offices to their homes and lock themselves in with their families and the streets at night are ghostly places were sometimes Syns prowl and kill—"

THERE WAS more—much more, for Ardyth had seemed to be pouring out the terror of her heart in that final letter, but it was all equally meaningless to Arthur Zoran. He had heard rumors of Syns from other sources in this final year. A group of workmen brought in from a job nearer home had carried with them stories of the terror that walked the streets of Earth's cities, particularly mid-western America where the thing seems to have started. They said that the term, Syn, was a corruption of Synthetic Men. But their stories were still second and third hand.

It sickened Arthur to think that this was what he and Ardyth would have surrounding them as they began their lives together. Most of all, it sickened him to think what it might have done to her. Her letters were as if she had forgotten every dream they had dreamed together. Not once—since that first time—had she mentioned the things they had planned, the white house, the great trees like those of Harold and Dorothy Weaver with whom she lived.

He would have brought Ardyth to Cyprian and signed on for another construction period, but even that had become impossible. A total ban against leaving Earth had been in effect for almost a year. Only the carefully screened crews of ships were allowed to leave, and Arthur had not seen any of these until three weeks ago. It was a series of long and unorganized hops from Earth to Cyprian II. Earth liners covered only half the distance. The rest of the way was by increasingly decrepit freighters and tubs of all kinds.

The crewmembers of the liner he was on were as close-mouthed as clams. He had exulted at the first sight of them and let go with all the questions he had bottled up for more than a year. They refused a single answer. His fellow passengers, coming home from scattered points of expatriation, were equally ignorant.

Burning sunlight advanced upon the port that looked into his room, and the automatic shades twisted to block out the invading rays and cast an ochre hue upon the air.

It was a sick dismal color, thought Arthur, the color of death. The color of the world to which he was going if he could believe but half of what he had heard.

He watched his hands resting upon his thighs. They looked like the hands of a mummy in that light. Shrunken and dehydrated by the long, unhealthful stay on Cyprian II, he was partly glad that Ardyth hadn't been permitted to come. He would not have wanted to see her become like himself, for it was the way all Earthmen became under those conditions.

THE ANNUNCIATOR chimed and a smooth baritone voice spoke in the room with sudden, gentle persuasion.

"All passengers will please come at once to the main dining salon. Instructions and preparations for landing must begin, and you are to be acquainted with the changes that have taken place upon Earth since you last saw it. This information is vital to everyone. Stewards will make a roll call and account for every passenger, so your cooperation and presence will be appreciated."

In the corridor, Arthur joined the other passengers slowly making their way toward the dining salon. There was little of shipboard gaiety among them. Through the journey their spirits had gradually dampened until a shroud of mutual hostility enfolded each like an invisible cocoon.

Arthur nodded to the few acquaintances he had. There was Ian McCarthy, a heavy, bronzed man of middle age, an explorer whose own ship had foundered many months ago and left him helpless until his accidental discovery. There were a couple of businessmen returning from extensive overseeing of their foreign properties.

These were about the sum of his acquaintances except for a slim figure of a girl who slipped into step beside him. When he became aware of her presence he did not know how long she had been there. She spoke suddenly in a frightened whisper of a voice, "It's about the Syns, isn't it?"

"I suppose so. I've never gone through anything like this before."

Her name was Jan Mercer, and she reminded him greatly of Ardyth with her small trim head of hair so neatly pressed into place. She had spoken to him frequently during the long days past, but he knew nothing of her.

"I wish I had never come back," she whispered.

He found them seats near the front of the room. He could not help noticing the trembling of her hands and lips.

"I had a friend, once, who was a Syn," she offered an explanation.

"Then you know! Tell me what it means—"

She shook her head. "You'll soon learn."

He wondered what kind of terrors this slender, frightened girl had seen. But he knew it was useless to press her for answers.

There was little murmuring among the passengers as they gathered. There were only three hundred of them, which was less than a third the capacity of the ship. The room felt cold although the temperature was adequate. It seemed as if already they were coming into the cloud of fear that hung about the Earth, its deepening mist sucking warmth and humanity out of them.

CAPTAIN TANNER, master of the vessel, rose before the group as the stewards reported the last of the passengers accounted for. He was a tall, gray-haired man whose face was lined not alone with age and responsibility of his profession but with a heavy regret as if he had somehow betrayed that profession by bringing them all back to Earth.

His voice was too low to be heard by those in the rear of the group, but all he said was. "Your response is appreciated, ladies and gentlemen. I present Captain Fairchild of Central Security, who has a message for you."

The CS man seemed the only one in the whole room who was sure of himself. He approached the speaker's point with the assurance of a military commander who knows that he, personally, does not have to meet the enemy. His florid face was grim and his voice ponderous.

"All of you here," he said, "have been away from Earth for more than a year. Since you have been away, few of you have learned more than rumors of the tragic events that have occurred in your absence. You have probably heard the term, Syn, in these rumors. Let me tell you what Syn means.

"Almost two years ago there came to one of our mental hospitals a patient with the fantastic story that he was not a human being, but an artificial production that had been turned out in one of the chemical research plants under Borg-K type logic-engine control. Routine analysis showed that this was not part of his insanity, but it was incredibly true. The punched molecules of his brain showed a variation and alteration that could not have come about in any known growth process. Electroencephalographs proved this. Their structure was analyzed thoroughly on the great Borg-K machine of the Allied Control Company. This confirmed the unbelievable story."

Arthur Zoran was startled as if a stranger had suddenly called his own name. Allied was the company for which he worked. The great Borg-K machine, which they called Eddie, was one he had helped build, at least in its expansions. And it was the logic-engine laboratory that he had supervised before leaving for Cyprian II.

"Not only did the logic engine show this man's story to be true," continued Fairchild, "it also revealed that many hundreds of thousands of these creatures of the same kind had been produced and turned loose among humanity. We learned how to identify them by an encephalogram analysis determined with the help of Allied's logic engine.

"The only thing we did not learn—and have not *yet* learned—is where these creatures are being produced. We know the how because we have actually duplicated the process with the aid of information provided by the logic engine. The creatures were given the name of Synthetic Men, and from this came Syn."

The room was hushed as if some alien thing had come into their midst and might have assumed the form of the person sitting next to each passenger. Arthur glanced at Jan Mercer. Her face was white and immobile.

"Each of you can guess in your own minds what this has meant on Earth," said the CS officer. These Syns have been moving steadily into human society, taking their places among men. Some have appeared as old men and women, others as young people, some as children. In ten thousand devious ways they have taken up life among us, even going to the extent of marrying human beings. And because of the destruction of population records during the War, it has not been suspected until now that these were not bona fide members of society. Ninety percent of the present population is without known filial relationships.

"The obvious and avowed purpose of the Syns is to replace humanity with what they consider a higher form of life. So far, they have given no evidence of intent to conquer by open warfare. But, like weeds growing in a garden, they hope to take over the entire garden for themselves.

"In every city of Earth we have set up inspection centers. Once a month the entire population is tested by electroencephalograph. Before you leave this ship each of you will be given such a test. In spite of the ban on travel from Earth, we picked up some Syns returning to Earth, having left before the ban.

"The human race will not be safe until these creatures are wiped out, until we destroy the reproduction centers from which they come. Our own technical organization is so complex that we have not been able to shut it down long enough or search deeply enough to find this source.

"It is a bitter world to which you are returning, and I offer no apology for it. The facilities of the entire world are concerned with the one task of destroying the Syns. If something of human dignity is being lost in the process—as you will find is the case—it is a small and temporary loss in order to wipe out this evil in our midst.

"If anyone doubts the urgency of this, consider for the moment: The man sitting next to you—the man or woman to whom you are married—any of these may be a Synthetic Man intent upon replacing and destroying you."

THE CS MAN sat down, and Captain Tanner stood again to give instructions in his tired voice for the testing of each passenger before landing.

Arthur Zoran scarcely heard this. He was still trying to digest the things that Fairchild had spoken. Arthur knew logic engines and factory controllers. That one of these should get out of kilter and start making artificial human beings was beyond his comprehension.

But the CS man believed it and, apparently, so did the rest of the world. There must be some additional truth somewhere that was as fantastic as this explanation, which he could scarcely force himself to accept.

The passengers rose and moved from the room. Each glanced more coldly and more fearfully at his neighbor than before as they made their way towards the privacy and security of the lonely cells.

Jan immediately lost herself in the crowd without a word to Arthur. He went alone to the solitary stateroom prison. There, he sat down on the bed and stared out at Earth's green disc. In the half million years since human forms of life appeared upon it, there had been spawned numberless and nameless kinds of horror. His parents and Ardyth's had known the War, and *their* grandparents likewise. But he wondered if any previous frightfulness had matched this one.

In that single moment as the group of passengers rose to leave the dining salon he felt a breath of hate exuding from each to all the rest. Past terrors had aligned men against men in mighty, evenly numbered divisions—but this put every man against every other.

He knew too well the vast potentialities of the controlling machines and logic engines, which he had helped build, to refuse acceptance of the story on the grounds of impossibility. Thousands of times the automatically controlled vats in the great chemical research centers duplicated the primal conditions of Earth's seas when sentient life first spawned in them. But for that vast process to be duplicated, a billion years of evolution compressed into months—there was the fantasy of it. In that, he could scarcely believe.

But yet he had to believe. The rumors of Syns and the story of the CS men would not turn out now to be dreams. The Syns existed. He put away his doubts and incredulity, and with full acceptance of this thing there came that terrible fear—what had it done to Ardyth?

He spent the next hours with preliminary packing, and when he was barely through he heard his name called for the encephalograph test.

There were a dozen or so in the line ahead of him. Jan Mercer was very near the head of it, but she did not look back—a dull, uniform fear was in the faces of each man and woman present. It was a *personal* thing, as if each in his own heart was no longer sure of their own identity.

After the test, Arthur returned to his stateroom. Timed by the Earth zone in which they would land, he spent a night period of restlessness.

Other passengers appeared to have done likewise, for they were on the promenade deck when he went out in the morning, their eyes drab with the failure of sleep.

He saw Jan coming down the deck; they headed for the same spot by the rail. She smiled now, and it made him remember the laughter of Ardyth. She looked more refreshed than at any time before, as if she had reached the low of her depression and had already begun the upward climb.

"It *will* be good to be home again," she said. "I should have never tried to run away, but I couldn't stand it after they took Jim—away. He was my husband—a Syn."

Arthur wished that she had prepared him for that. He wished for some preliminary remark before the sudden unveiling of that naked insight into the desolation that lay below them. It caught his breath and made his lungs ache in a moment of inexpressible pity.

Her eyelashes were quite wet now, and he saw that despite the smile they had scarcely dried since she last cried.

"What—happened?" he murmured.

"What happens to all of them? Killed—slaughtered like some animal. They were wrong. Jim was human and real. I tell you there's something terribly wrong down there on Earth. They haven't found the answer yet. I don't know about the rest of the Syns, but I know my Jim was real…"

Arthur put his arm about her shoulders to help control the sudden trembling that had again possessed her. His hand encountered another touch that he instinctively judged as brutal. He quickly looked around. Captain Fairchild and another CS man were standing behind, reaching for Jan.

"We want to see you, Mrs. Mercer. Will you please come to your cabin at once?"

The girl turned. At the sight of the men she screamed once. Other passengers gathered quickly, comprehending the significance of the CS men. They closed about with predatory expectancy that relieved for the moment the pressure upon their own minds.

Arthur felt suddenly sick and yearned to smash the nearest of those animal faces, but Fairchild's assistant was pushing them back with impatient snarls.

"Please come," repeated Fairchild, jerking at Jan's arm.

She held back and turned again to Arthur. "I told you," she murmured, and now her face seemed lighted with a great expectancy and relief.

"I told you they were wrong and hadn't found the answer—but *this* is *my* answer! This is why nothing seemed right after Jim was taken. He's been waiting for me. He knew I'd soon be coming!"

CHAPTER TWO

THERE WERE none of the gay crowds at the dock. It was like a landing at a ghost city of Mars, where only scattered handfuls of men skulked between half-abandoned buildings in nameless pursuits.

At the edge of the field, no more than a mile away, were the skeletal ruins of Old Town, the city destroyed by the War, its scars not yet erased by the new generation.

Baggage handlers moved up to the ships. There were tiny knots of people huddled by the pillars under the roof of the pier watching anxiously as the passengers streamed from the ship through three separate ports.

At each pier gate three CS men stood in ominous guardianship. They examined the card that each passenger had to present, showing he had passed the test aboard ship, proving his humanity.

As if he might be an enemy of his own country Arthur received grim permission to pass.

"Don't lose that card, buddy," one guard said. "It's as much as your life is worth to be without one."

This ominous warning was scarcely heard, lost in the urgency with which his eyes searched the dock for Ardyth. She would be there to welcome him. But she was not a part of the tiny knot of people beside the nearest column. He ran the whole length of the pier. Within minutes, he knew that she was not present on the almost barren landing area.

Through the doors of the port building he went out to the street. At midday this looked half-deserted, and its desolation was all the greater for Ardyth's absence.

She worked in a laboratory. He knew the idiosyncrasies of lab directors. Maybe she had been refused leave. But she would be off in a couple of hours. He would go to Harold and Dorothy Weaver's house, where Ardyth lived.

Because she had no family of her own, Ardyth Crane boarded with the Weavers in their own home. Arthur took a waiting cab and was soon riding through the familiar streets.

On every side was the same persistent lifelessness. It had the look of a city built for a million and inhabited by a thousand or two.

"Looks bad, huh?" The driver was watching his face.

"You'd think some disease had wiped out half the population and sickened the rest," said Arthur.

"Yeah, I never seen anybody get off a ship yet that didn't wish he could get right back on and go back to the place where he came from. If they didn't have the ban on, I'd have gone long ago and so would most everybody else."

He pulled up in front of the Weavers' and let Arthur out.

THE WEAVERS had the kind of place that Arthur and Ardyth had dreamed of owning for themselves. There was a wide, rambling white house set in big grounds surrounded by trees. On the grass beside the house he saw now the figure of Sally, the five-year-old Weaver, but no—she *had* been five. She would be seven now, he thought. He wondered if she would remember.

"Hi, Sally," he called.

The child looked up with a frightened glance, and then, screaming loudly, she ran to the rear of the house.

Arthur went up to the front door and knocked. He could hear the commotion of Sally's sobbing cries inside, and then footsteps approaching the door.

"Hello, Dorothy. I'm sorry I gave Sally such a fright. She couldn't have recognized me after I've been on Cyprian for so long."

"Arthur—!"

It was not an exclamation of welcome. His smile faded as he tried to understand what was in Dorothy Weaver's voice as she spoke his name. Then he had it. Dismay.

She was a heavy, auburn-haired woman who had always had a ready laugh upon her lips, but she had changed in a kind of horrible way. She had lost much weight and her flesh seemed to have sagged without shrinking. Her face looked as if she had not smiled for a very long time.

"Arthur—" she repeated as if in a daze. "I had almost forgotten—Wait just a moment and I'll call Harold."

Carefully she closed the door, leaving him standing outside. The spring wind in the trees felt suddenly cold.

If the Syn hunt had done this to gay Dorothy, what might it have done to his serious, wondering, little Ardyth? He felt a quick panic as if he had to see her that very instant. He almost turned to flee down the walk and find Ardyth where she worked, but the door opened suddenly and Harold Weaver stepped out.

"Hello, Arthur, I'm glad you're back," he said. But in his eyes there was no welcome. "You'll have to excuse Dorothy. We just weren't looking for you, that's all. We can't let you stay more than a minute, but come in and sit down for that long, anyway."

"Yeah—yeah, sure." Arthur picked up his bag and followed Harold into the house. Harold was a thin, bony man of intense energies, but that energy seemed to have been drained out of him. Of friendship there was none; yet once they had been very close.

"I'm sorry about Sally," said Arthur as they sat upon a sofa. "I didn't think I'd scare her even if I had been away so long."

"It's not that." Harold passed a hand over his forehead in a helpless gesture. "It's just all of *this*— We've told her not to speak to anyone—made her afraid to. The sight of a stranger terrifies her since—"

Suddenly he looked up with helpless terror in his eyes. He glanced from Arthur to the doorway leading to the rear of the house. Dorothy was coming in, the trembling Sally beside her.

"Dorothy—" Harold gasped. "Arthur doesn't—*can't* know—"

Then Arthur heard his own voice rising in fear. "What is it? Ardyth—has anything happened to her?"

Dorothy spoke flatly as if beyond all shock, all fear. "She's a Syn, didn't you know?"

IT was not the face of Ardyth whose image exploded in his mind. Rather, that of terrified Jan Mercer when the CS men took her by the arm and she had cried, "I told you they were wrong and hadn't found the answer—"

They had taken her away to be destroyed like an animal marauder.

"Ardyth—" His voice broke with panic. "They killed her—"

"No," said Dorothy. "She got away. When they think they're about to be discovered lots of the Syns escape. They're clever."

"But you don't believe she was a Syn!" he cried. "Not Ardyth! She was clean, and sweet—and human!"

"Be careful what you say," advised Dorothy. "They've caught a lot of them just by inference and friendship with other Syns. We've got to ask you to go now. They'll be here asking to see our cards again and submit to a special check, just because you came, because you knew Ardyth—"

He tried to find words that would bridge the gap between them. He looked to Harold, but the man only returned his glance helplessly. There was nothing left of the friends he had once known. They were drained to mere husks that bore only the names of the friends he had expected to find.

He got up, his eyes glancing slowly about the room. Here in this house he and Ardyth had known mad, happy times. Here he had made love to her and she had answered his proposal with a promise to marry him. And Harold and Dorothy had been almost as happy at the news as Arthur and Ardyth themselves.

Now Ardyth was gone—dead or worse. And the Weavers had become servants of fear.

"I'll be going," he whispered in hoarse tones that did not seem to be his own voice.

Neither of the others spoke. He moved to the door alone. Only when he opened it did they see the car outside and the men advancing towards the house. Arthur looked inquiringly at Harold. Dorothy had already rushed to the window, tearing aside the shades.

"They're here again. What can they want this time? Why don't they leave us alone?"

Two heavy-set men with bleak, friendless faces came into the room as Arthur held the door.

"We've had our monthly examinations and our specials!" cried Dorothy. "We've got our cards. What more do you want of us? Why don't you go away and leave us alone?"

"Take it easy, lady," said one of the CS men. "We're only doing what's necessary. You have a Sally Weaver here?"

Dorothy's face went white with shock. "Sally's our daughter. Leave her alone. Don't you touch her—"

"We have the encephalogram report of Sally Weaver. This was her first, it is indicated. The report is that Sally Weaver is not human. She must be released to us for further testing and disposal."

Harold rose now, his step like that of an old man sick with the cold of age and death's white breath.

"Sally's our daughter. You can't take our Sally—"

"Not your flesh and blood daughter. You adopted her. Is that not true?"

"Yes—yes, but she's like our own. Sally's human, we *know*. Don't you think we'd know if she was some monster?"

"No. No one knows." He looked at the spindly girl who clung behind Dorothy, her arms encircling the woman's wide hips.

The bleak face seemed to sag momentarily in lines of infinite weariness. *"We're* human, too," he said.

"Not if you take our little girl away from us!" cried Harold. "Get out of this house!"

"Be careful, please," the CS man warned. He reached for the thin arm of Sally Weaver.

Dorothy backed quickly as if shrinking from a cobra's thrust. The officer caught Sally's arm and dragged her away.

For the first time then, she screamed. The cry was a shriller, deeper sound than the ear could endure. A wire knife, it cut through the toughest tissues with ruthless shearing.

"Mommy—don't let them take me! What are they going to do to me, Mommy?"

The fear and terror instilled in her since the discovery of the Syns now bloomed in horrible fruitfulness.

The CS men raged at their own instincts for tenderness towards this thing that was a monster instead of a human. They jerked her roughly through the door. The slamming of it muffled her screams and gave the illusion of sudden distance as if already she was beyond human reach. And all up and down the street mothers crouched in terror by their windows, wondering if their house would be the next stop of the CS car.

Arthur became aware that the scene had passed and he had not uttered a sound. It seemed in fact as if he had witnessed only a reproduction of something that could not possibly have any connection with reality. In a moment someone would appear on the stage and sign the players off and tell him the fantasy was ended.

But Dorothy was huddled on the floor where she had fallen. Soundless sobbing shook the arch of her back. Slowly, she raised a hand and touched Arthur's knee.

"Help us, Arthur," she begged. "Help us get our Sally back. Help us find a way, please—"

CHAPTER THREE

HE WALKED most of the afternoon, walked the near empty streets of the city, and watched the occasional faces of figures that passed with bent, contracted stride as if against a blast of winter's wind.

Eyes glanced hastily at him from these faces, shying even from this faint contact with another human being, turning away to loneliness and the security of solitude.

Where in all of heaven or hell lay the answer to this ghastly mess he demanded fiercely of the unhearing silence of the city? Where was Ardyth—hiding in lonely terror from the merciless death that stalked her? He had to know—he had to find Ardyth if she still lived, and he'd kill the man who'd harmed her.

She was no Syn—not Ardyth of the warm lips and laughing eyes.

"We'll have a house just like Harold and Dorothy's," she'd said, "only bigger, to hold three boys and three girls. And when you become very famous you'll have to grow a long, black beard so everyone will know it, because they won't believe that a nice, simple guy like you could be such a noted scientist."

But what if she actually was a Syn? How much difference would that make? The answer was simple. As far as he was concerned, she was as human as anyone he had ever known. If she had been created by a process of evolution that paralleled man's it made little difference that it had begun in a chemical vat instead of a hot, slimy sea.

If she were a Syn, then there was no practical distinction between men and Syns. Wherever she was hiding, he'd find her, and he'd bring her back and defy the whole world to harm or reject her. If the Syns and men had no common ancestor there was no cause for their being unable to live together. There could be peace between them. There *would* be peace, he swore bitterly.

A vow to find Ardyth was easier taken than carried out. Obviously, the murderous forces of Central Security were scouring the city for escaped Syns. If they had failed so far to find her, how could he go about it, and in secret, too, so that he would not lead them to her?

There was an answer to that.

Eddie.

At the thought of the great logic engine he felt a warmth as if at the mention of the name of an old and dear friend. And that is exactly the way it was. The machine was his friend, closer now, he thought, than the present race of humans that had turned to incomprehensible brutality in his absence, that had become the willing murderers of innocent Jan and Sally, and that had sought the life of the woman he loved.

Eddie would understand these things. He operated only on a basis of clear, logical truth with infallible accuracy. He did not know the erratic emotional inconsistency of human beings.

It was not strange to think of the machine as a friend. Before he went to Cyprian II, Arthur had been in charge of Eddie for a year, and he had gained more skill in manipulation of the engine than anyone else. He had been jokingly accused of building into it a dog-like sense of devotion based on olfactory principles. But his fellow technicians at Allied had long recognized that he could get more and clearer results from Eddie than anyone else could.

Arthur had told Eddie about his engagement to Ardyth. He had consulted the engine about the trip to Cyprian II, and had based his final decision largely on Eddie's recommendations.

This, however, was strictly an illegal proceeding because the engine's time was so consumed by questions of worldwide import that private inquiry was strictly taboo. Everything entering the machine was recorded, and Arthur had had to lock the recorder when using only for personal reasons.

Finding Ardyth now was more than personal, he thought. Establishing peace between men and Syns was of cosmic importance. It might be difficult to convince Dr. Waldron, Allied's Scientific Director, of this, however. If so, he'd have to find some obscure way to get access to Eddie again.

While these thoughts passed through his mind, he had been walking steadily and rapidly in the direction of the plant, and now he came up before the high fence and steel gates that opened onto the grounds of the vast organization.

THE GRAY mass of the building hardly looked more inviting than the rest of the frightened and dying city. He almost dreaded to enter it for fear that all his former friends would be as Harold and Dorothy Weaver—or as Ardyth.

The receptionist was away from her desk as he entered the front door, so he encountered no one until he reached his own laboratory, which he had formerly directed. He opened the door of the office that had once been his.

A white-haired man in a laboratory coat was sitting at the desk. He looked up suddenly and then his face broke into a warm and cordial smile. He advanced with outstretched hand.

"Arthur...it's wonderful to see you again. I'd forgotten your ship was in today. We'd have sent someone down—"

"That's all right, Doc. I didn't expect a welcoming committee." He pumped the man's hand with a fierce grip. Doc Trainer was little changed from the way he had appeared when Arthur left. The same warm humanity seemed in him instead of being drained out as with all the others.

"Sit down," he invited, "and tell me all about the horrors of Cyprian."

"They couldn't begin to match those of Earth," said Arthur flatly.

Trainer's smile died, and now Arthur was aware that Doc had not escaped, after all—

"What's it all about?" he pleaded suddenly. "It's got Ardyth. I went by Weavers' and they told me she was a Syn. I've got to find her. What crazy thing has happened to the world since I left?"

"I didn't know—I didn't know about Ardyth. I'm terribly sorry for you, Arthur."

"Tell me what is the answer to all this."

"I wish I could. I wish *someone* knew."

"This story of the Syns…it's a crazy thing! How could a chemical machine go off its base and start making artificial people? That's insane."

"It is—completely insane—and implacably true."

"Ardyth was as human as you or I, and so is little Sally Weaver, but they're going to kill her—murder that child in cold blood because of this wave of insanity that has swept the world."

Arthur's face took on a look of astonishment, as if in this moment he comprehended anew the magnitude of tragedy. "It's like the ancient tales of Salem witchcraft, where the pointing finger of a jealous neurotic could destroy any innocent person. That's what this whole thing is—nothing more than a gigantic, worldwide witch hunt!"

Doc Trainer looked suddenly about, then crossed and closed the door leading into the outer laboratory. "The first thing that you've got to learn," he said grimly, "is to stop making statements like that. In one respect this is like a witch-hunt. Everywhere are prying ears of sick, jealous humans who will report such remarks as you made, and the CS will act on them, demanding your reexamination."

Trainer shook his head sadly. "But that's as far as the similarity goes. I wish it were only a Salem witch-hunt. But the Syns are real. You can ask Eddie for yourself. He is chiefly responsible for our understanding of the problem. He gave us the encephalograph test by which we uncover the Syns."

"Then why can't he tell you how and where they are made?"

"He has told us how, and we have actually duplicated the process and have made some for ourselves. So we know it can and is being done. But he can't tell us where, as you can obviously understand. He doesn't have the data and can't possibly extrapolate it any more than we can."

"I wonder..." said Arthur slowly. "It seems to me that he has a good deal of the essential data—"

"You'd better go on up and see Waldron right away. He's got something pretty urgent for you. It has to do with the Syns. CS has taken Eddie over to work exclusively on it, and Waldron thinks you and Eddie may be able to work it out together."

Sudden relief flowed through Arthur's mind. This was better than anything he had hoped for—being reassigned to Eddie!

"Thanks. I'll go right up."

DR. WALDRON was a scientific executive whose knowledge of a dozen fields was nearly encyclopedic in its magnitude, and whose handling of his organization was as impartial as the judgments of an engineer driving a great machine.

Arthur sometimes thought he was part of the great machine that was Allied Control, and almost looked for the invisible wiring that must connect the Director with the machines of the plant.

Dr. Waldron glanced up sharply as his secretary announced Arthur and led him in. He then advanced over and shook hands firmly, his black eyes scanning Arthur from head to foot as if judging his fitness for further use.

"That was an excellent piece of work you turned out on Cyprian," he said. "We are glad you are back, however. There's a serious project that I want to assign to you. Sit down and I'll tell you about it."

He punched the interphone buttons and leaned forward to the mike. "Please ask Mr. Benson and Mr. Trask to come in."

Benson and Trask; they were new names that meant nothing to Arthur. He felt they were of no concern to him. He didn't want to know anybody named Trask and Benson. He wished that Waldron would ask him just one personal question—how was Ardyth? When did he plan to marry her—?"

Two men entered the office while he considered these bitter opinions of Waldron. The Director introduced them.

"This is Mr. Arthur Zoran, our logic-engine specialist. Arthur, these are Mr. Trask and Mr. Benson of Central Security. You are to work with them during the course of your next assignment."

The men nodded stiff greetings while rage surged high through Arthur's mind. He almost blurted out the turmoil of his feelings as he thought of the other CS men he had seen in recent days—their hands snatching at Jan Mercer, tearing poor Sally Weaver from her mother's arms—

He held back the words and returned only their greetings—with equal stiffness. Only Dr. Waldron seemed as if the world were as it should be. But his words now belied this.

"How much do you know about the Syns, Arthur?" he asked.

Briefly, Arthur repeated the things he had been told, omitting the actual incidents of his previous encounters with CS.

Dr. Waldron nodded when he had finished. "You know now about as much as do any of us who have lived with and fought this thing for the past year or two.

"Allied Control has been given a top priority contract to work with CS on the solution of this situation. We've spent a large amount of time on it—mostly without results. I want you to take over the project because you and Eddie work as a team that can't be matched anywhere else in our organization. Doc Trainer can assist if you like."

"Where am I expected to begin?"

"You're on your own. Pick your lab crew to suit yourself. Call for any facilities you need, never mind the cost. You have a blank check. We ask only that you immediately report any conclusions on possible lines of action."

"We've got to know where the location is that the Syns hide out in," said Trask as if this thought were the end product of vast cogitation. "And we've got to know where they have set up their reproduction centers. Those are the two most important things we need to know. Supply us with that information, and we'll do the rest to wipe them out."

HE COULDN'T talk to these men, Arthur realized. He couldn't ask anyone of them why Sally Weaver and Jan Mercer had to die. They would stare at him with horrible suspicion—and demand that he have a recheck.

The wall between him and the other men was ever thickening and growing higher.

But inside, he felt a sudden, overwhelming feeling of joyous exultation. As far as solving his own problem was concerned, they were practically offering him the whole plant.

"Is this wholly agreeable with you?" asked Dr. Waldron.

Arthur nodded. "I've seen enough since I got back to make me willing to put all my effort into such a project. The first thing I'd like is a transcript of all news items and official reports on the subject since the Syns were discovered."

Waldron nodded. "They are already available. I have them here for you. Most of the material, however, has already been put into Eddie. He can give it to you quicker than you can read it."

Arthur spent the remainder of the late afternoon locating an apartment for himself and poring over some of the various news materials with which he had been provided.

In the reports and editorials there was a universal flame of fanaticism and pseudo-religious zeal to promote the destruction of the Syns.

In that lay the greatest horror of all, he thought. It wasn't merely that the Syns were so much like normal humans and were systematically being hunted down and killed. It was the sudden release of worldwide bloodlust, violence, and mayhem. Each man who reported or editorialized on the Syns seemed to have become a vessel of wrath calling for the blood of these creatures as if it were some high and sacred duty instead of a loathsome necessity.

Humanity was horrified by the events, and even while they were sick with that horror, they lusted in it. He recalled the faces of those who had gathered about Jan Mercer on the space liner when the CS men captured her. Wild dogs awaiting the kill.

He lay back on the bed, watching the twilight close over the city of despair.

How could he convince such men that there must be peace between Syns and humans?

When it was done, perhaps then the reproductive plants could be dismantled and eventually the Syns would die out and their advent be only a ghastly interval in the history of humanity.

Or—perhaps something good would come, something lasting and fine, something more than these brutal killers called humans deserved.

CHAPTER FOUR

HE COULDN'T sleep. The imaginative night-things of all the ages winged their shadowy way across the city and past each open window. He dreamed he saw them perching on the sill with flaming eyes and ravenous beaks. He heard the ancient witch cries from far across time, and saw the helpless witches of Salem beaten and tortured by men of his own kind, killed in bloody self-righteousness.

Then he raised up and went to the window and understood that those cries were not of fantasy and dreaming. They were real, coming from some distant nucleus of despair down in the city.

Sleep could not be won on this brink of hell. He dressed and went out into the cool night air. He took his own car, which he had recovered from storage, and drove to the silent plant of Allied Control.

It was dark now except for the occasional night light of a watchman. He rang the bell and waited during the long interval still hearing the distant cry in the city until the watchman came to let him in.

He went directly to the laboratory that housed Eddie, and turned on the lights. The great logic engine was a fantastic thing in the night, but to Arthur it was like an old friend on whose shoulder he could lean in complete trust.

Of them all, Eddie was the one creature in whom sanity remained. Arthur walked slowly past the long, familiar panels. Black and expressionless, they were dotted here and there with meters and inspection windows.

These hundreds of feet of paneling banked high with millions of components formed the most powerful logic engine ever built. It had personality; it had idiosyncrasies that made it an individual. There was no question whatever that it could think.

It was Eddie.

It was a far cry from the anthropomorphic automatons that had preceded Eddie's forbears in men's imagination, but it had powers greater than ever dreamed for those crude tin men.

Arthur opened the door of the control room and sat down at the operating panel. He flipped the master switch.

"Hi, Eddie," he said.

The scanning eyes in front of him seemed almost to blink with surprise, but he knew it was only the adjusting voltage being brought up to properly record his darkened skin.

"Arthur—"

The voice was a pleasant baritone. As in the case of an unseen speaker over radio or telephone, Arthur had imagined long ago the kind of person Eddie would be. He imagined a young engineer about his own age, lean and competent, with a sense of humor matured beyond all childishness. Eddie, as he imagined him, was the kind of a person who would have been his most intimate friend in the flesh.

"Why didn't you come in sooner?" The sound came from the black core of a speaker mounted beside the eyes. "I thought you'd drop in the instant you arrived."

"I wanted to see about Ardyth first. Can't you understand that?"

"Of course. I thought you might have found out earlier. You know now, of course, that she was found to be a Syn."

"Yes. They told me she escaped. As far as I know she is still alive and I've got to find her. Can you help me, Eddie?"

"What do you want me to do? What if she is alive and you do bring her back? She'll be killed."

"Eddie—what is the difference between a Syn and a human? Is there any at all except in the matter of parentage?"

"None. Except that the Syns may be a little more sane than your kind."

"Then why can't they live together? Waldron and the officers of Central Security want me and you to figure out how to locate and destroy both the Syns and their reproduction centers. I don't think it is necessary. I think some way could be found to declare peace between the two groups."

"Yes, they've tried for weeks to force me to extrapolate from data I don't have. They mentioned you would be in and that we would be assigned the task of seeing to the Syns' destruction.

"As for your question, you know your own people well enough to answer that. When have they ever al-lowed a divergent minority to live in peace? Your religious history reeks with betrayal, slaughter, holy wars, oppression of disbelievers and unorthodox believers. For four thousand years you have cried peace and unity and tried to enforce it on a community scale, but you have never understood that until each man achieves his own private tolerance that there can be no brotherly love or peace.

"The answer is 'no'—without any qualifications whatever. The Syns can *not* live among you in peace. There is no community of your people upon the whole Earth that would accept them. The most merciful thing that can be done is to carry out the eradication program already begun. Your own personal tragedy would be multiplied ten thousand times if you should ever see Ardyth again. I advise you not to search."

"You're a monster," said Arthur fervently. "You may be the greatest accumulation of brain stuff ever put together on Earth, but there's one thing that you haven't got."

"What is that?"

"Hope."

FOR A LONG time there was absolute silence from the machine. Another operator would have begun to glance aside at the myriad dials and panel lights for indications of breakdown, but Arthur knew Eddie.

He could sense the wave of impulses exploding to the farthest depths of the machine, rebounding and echoing back at the speed of light, searching through the tapes and memory pots for an understanding of the single word that Arthur had spoken.

Then Eddie answered.

"I have no hope. I understand the term only in connection with human beings, and humans characterized by hope are characterized by irrational expectancies based upon mere desire, which has no correlation with probability. I see no value in the quality mentioned."

"You never will, Eddie. You'll never know what hope is because it's the thing that makes me a man, and lack of it that makes you nothing but a damned machine that can sit there and tell me to never search for the girl I love."

The machine was silent again for a long time, and then there came a sound that seemed uttered in the depths of bitterness—and Arthur knew the impression was insane even as he felt it, but he could not shake it off.

"Love, too," said Eddie, "is characterized by irrational expectancies and desires not related to probability."

Then Arthur laughed out loud. "Eddie, you're nothing but a damned old cynic. Now listen, we've got work to do. Get busy and figure me out a course of action. First, I must locate Ardyth. I have hope that Syns and humans can live together in peace. I'm going to work to that end. In order to maintain my position here, I've got to go through the motions of trying to find the Syns who have escaped and the reproduction centers they've set up.

"With those requirements, I want to know the best course of action follow. Is that clear?"

"Clear, but hardly logical. You will fail on both counts and end up in dismissal from your position here and with a personal tragedy involving Ardyth that cannot be described in the logical terms at my disposal."

"I'll take a chance on it. Shift into high, and give me the dope."

The machine waited as if in reluctance, and this time Arthur did look at the indicator panel. The seeming hesitancy was not in accordance with the design characteristics of the machine. Reluctance implied will and desires, which the machine certainly did not have, in spite of the human personality with which it was endowed—or which Arthur had imagined into it.

There was no indication of improper operation, however. The lights were green where they should be green and blank where blanks should be. No red appeared at all.

Then suddenly the machine resumed speaking. "The probability is very high," it said, "that you can find Ardyth if you contact the Syns, letting them think that you are one of them. This will involve no discrepancy because they automatically accept any who are rejected by humans. They could, but chose not to make use of the electroencephalograph."

"How may I contact them?"

"Permit yourself to be treated as one of them. Arrange a scene with officers of Central Security in which you are pursued as a Syn, but allowed to escape. There is an underground organization of Syns of great complexity. They have scattered posts in the city through which they assist such escapes and provide refuge. Let your false pursuit extend over a wide area in those sections near Old Town, and you will be almost certain to encounter a member of the Syn underground who will give you refuge—and eventually lead you to Ardyth."

"Then what?"

"Then what? Then you will marry her and you will go on with your scheme to promote peace between the two groups. In the ensuing conflict, you will be killed."

IT WAS Arthur who paused now without speaking. The voice of the machine was suddenly not his friend, Eddie, the logic engine, but some portentous oracle of doom that he could not defy.

Eddie's statements were not one hundred percent accurate prophecies because Eddie did not have all the data, all the variables that would enter the picture as events moved on. But within the limits of his information, he was infallible.

"Run through it again, Eddie," said Arthur in a low voice. "Find another alternative."

"It won't do any good. I gave it to you the way it comes out."

"Come on. Try it."

There was a brief moment of silence, then the voice of the machine boomed. "There is no alternative; I have given you the only possibilities."

"All right," said Arthur wearily, "I'll take a chance on the variables that you don't know."

"I'll not likely be seeing you again, then," said Eddie. "Goodbye."

It was stupid, he thought, standing there saying goodbye to a machine, but he said it. "Bye, Eddie."

He got in his car and drove away from the silent plant. Through the dark streets of the city the lights of his car moved like the flash beam of some archeologist penetrating the halls of a long dead and forgotten city of ancient times.

He was a fool, he thought, to consider any other course than the infallible program that Eddie had formulated. Kill the Syns—wipe out their breeding centers.

Abandon hope of Ardyth—

Eddie couldn't lie.

But men did not live by infallible logic. They had to live by faith and hope, which the emotionless brain of Eddie pronounced futile. If they ever abandoned those qualities they would be no more than Eddie—mere machines.

From the moment that men first suspected their giant creations of thinking ability, they had feared these brains of metal and glass and streaming electrons, feared them because giant brains like Eddie could never understand that Arthur Zoran had to find the girl he loved—and die in the attempt if that were the requirements of Eddie's unanswerable logic.

Arthur knew Eddie had given him the best possible course of action under the circumstances. He would follow it as closely as possible—and hope to avoid the bitter consequences Eddie predicted.

At dawn he was awake after brief hours of sleep. He went directly to the plant again and called for a conference with Trask and Benson and Waldron. There he outlined the plan Eddie had given him—omitting the restrictions he had imposed upon the logic engine. The CS officers were not impressed.

"We've tried that," said Trask somewhat scornfully. "In every one of a hundred cities we've followed and traced down Syns who have tried to escape. Some of them we even deliberately let go in order to find their hiding places, just as you propose to do. It never got us anywhere."

"Did you ever let one of your own men go in the manner Eddie suggests?"

"No. There are two reasons why that plan is foolish. In the first place, if we ever tried such a thing the mobs would kill the person before he got halfway."

"But some of the Syns do escape."

"Not often. Once you got among the Syns and they suspected the slightest thing wrong, they'd kill you instantly. And don't think for a minute that they aren't smart enough to find out.

"It's all right with me if you want to risk your neck. We'll cooperate, but you haven't got a chance."

He should have added: That's what Eddie believes, too, Arthur thought, but he merely nodded agreement. "You make the arrangements for me to be tested negatively and provide for some means of escape. I'll do the rest."

CHAPTER FIVE

IT WAS like a great cattle pen. A mass of dejected humanity was crowded into the ugly red stone building housing the CS test program for the city.

Arthur took his place in the long line. Far ahead of him, rough wooden seats were provided against the dirty walls, but a hundred slumped and beaten human forms intervened between him and those seats. A hundred symbols of defeat. Some sat upon the floor their legs straight out before them. Others hunkered up with heads buried against their knees. And each shifted with a grotesque wriggle of his body as the line moved a step nearer to the point where some would be freed to return to life, and others condemned to ruthless slaughter.

Those who were not sitting on the floor leaned dejectedly against the wall, sliding along it, insistent upon its support, as if they could no longer bear the weight of their own existence.

There was dirt. It was upon the walls where they had leaned and slid along. It was upon the floor where they had scuffed their feet and spat in helpless anger. And it was upon their own persons.

Cattle, Arthur thought. To each of them, who had come once a month for almost two long years, seeing each time more of their numbers consigned to slaughter, it must seem as if they would all be taken if only they came often enough. They were already condemned. It was only a matter of time until their own personal sentence was read.

There were children in the mob, too, lively little children like Sally Weaver, coming for the first time. And some of these would not leave the building this day or else would be recalled with cruel persistence as Sally had been.

He wondered what would happen if he should call for the opinion and vote of these on the question of establishing peace with the Syns. Would there be any one of these beaten cattle who would refuse a place to the rejected ones when he, himself, might be the next to receive the thumbs down mark of the gods' disfavor?

He did not understand how it was that some of the Syns could pass the test month after month and be caught only after twenty or thirty testings. It was the defect in the testing procedure, Waldron had explained. Being improved constantly, the test was still far from perfect. They leaned over backwards to make sure that no real humans were branded as Syns.

They had told him that a Syn knew his own nature, of course, but if this was true, Arthur could not understand why they simply came to the testing rooms time after time, gambling indefinitely on their uncertain ability to pass. Why didn't they segregate themselves to escape this slaughter?

This was not their purpose, Waldron had explained. Their purpose was to infiltrate and take over human affairs, not to segregate themselves. Besides, they were only damned machines. They had no emotion of hope or yearning for life. Destruction meant nothing to them, individually.

But always, Arthur's criterion was Ardyth.

Ardyth—a machine? Without emotion, without love of life?

Arthur cursed softly to himself. Somewhere they had overlooked some great and important truths about the nature of Syns. He didn't believe Syns actually knew their own natures.

THE MAN in front of him in line had been talking in spasmodic grunts since Arthur came in. Some of his muttering finally entered Arthur's consciousness.

"Nobody comes to buy anything anymore," the little fat man was saying. "Another month like the last one and I'll have to close up. Then what'll happen? I ask you where'll I be then, with my store closed up? These stinking Syns—I wish I could get a couple for myself."

"Are you sure that you will always be able to pass the test?" said Arthur.

The man turned slowly as if Arthur had called him a dirty name. "What do you mean by that?" he demanded. "Who're you calling a lousy Syn?"

"No one," said Arthur. "But I just wondered how it is that some of us go through and pass the test maybe nine times and on the tenth one are rejected."

"That's because the lousy Syns are so damned clever. They know how to fake their way through the test, but sooner or later they'll all be caught and then the world will get back to normal. If I could only get me a few of them before then," he finished savagely.

Arthur understood their brutality now. Each one believed that *he*, personally, could pass the test forever. But was it true?

"Don't you think it possible that we could live with them?" he said. "Do they really have to be killed?"

The man stared at Arthur as if unable to believe his senses. "You talk like one of them! If I thought you were—"

"No—I've been away for a long time. This is my first test since I got off the ship. I don't know what it's been like living with the Syns loose, but it seemed there ought to be an easier way than all this killing."

"Smashing a lousy machine that's gone mad is not killing. Damn, I'll bet you *are* one of the things, after all. You talk just like one."

By now, others had overheard the conversation, and the little fat merchant turned grinning to them. Don't he talk just like one of them? I'll bet he don't get through the test."

There was sage nodding of agreement.

My brothers. My fellow men! Arthur thought—

A man behind him spoke with some show of kindness. "I just wouldn't talk like that if I were you, buddy. It's not safe—"

"Move along there you guys!" There came the impatient snarls of offended humanity anxious to close the gap that had appeared in the line ahead of Arthur and the merchant. Humanity anxious to have its chance to be tested for damnation, he thought.

It was nightfall when Arthur finally reached the inner sanctum. The technicians had been notified by CS of the plan, but they did not even glance at him as he entered. One of them at a desk was at the panel of a huge punched-card machine.

"Card," he demanded.

"I'm Arthur Zoran."

"Card, please!"

"Arthur Zoran of CS."

The apathetic technician looked up as if unsettled by this interruption of routine.

"Arthur Zoran—oh yes."

He turned away to confer hastily with an older man at the testing equipment. The latter straightened and approached Arthur. His smile was utterly bleak as if there could be no humor or good feeling whatever within the confines of this building.

"We are ready for you, Mr. Zoran," he said. "We hope you are successful."

HE LED the way through an adjacent door to a barren chamber. Inside, he looked about with a puzzled air. "Strange. They must have taken that other fellow out. They told me the euthanasia chamber was full. We had a Syn here just before you that gave the strongest reaction we have seen for a long time. He was manacled to this ring on the wall.

"Anyway, you are to go out that door that I have just unlocked, across the room. Follow straight down the hall. A car has been left outside. Follow the driveway on out. The guards have instructions to let you pass without question. Two minutes after you leave the grounds the alarm will be sounded in the city signifying the escape of a Syn. After that, you are on your own."

"Thank you," Arthur shook hands with the doctor and watched him disappear back into the testing room.

For an instant, Arthur stood surveying the dirty anteroom to death. Little Sally Weaver must have passed through here, and before her, countless thousands had passed this way going to the euthanasia chamber because they lacked the same kind of humanity as those who judged them.

He shook off the sick pall of fear that exuded from the very walls and approached the door that had been indicated.

He opened it cautiously. Then from out of the dimness of the poorly lit hall a squat, snarling figure hurled itself upon him. Desperate, pudgy fingers wrapped about his throat seeking to encase his neck in a strangling hold.

The assailant was hardly a match for Arthur, his body thin and wire-hard from his years on Cyprian. His own fingers twisted on one fat wrist with crushing force. The grip about his throat disappeared as his enemy twisted away with a cry of pain. Arthur spun him to the floor in a crushing fall that knocked the breath from him.

He lay there groaning and whimpering without rising. It was the blustering merchant who had stood in line all day ahead of Arthur.

Viciously, Arthur spoke, "I guess you were right. Syns are pretty smart, getting through the tests for months—but they finally get caught, don't they?"

"I'm not a Syn," the man blubbered. "They made a mistake somehow. I tell you I'm not a lousy Syn!"

"You'd like to get yourself a couple before this is over, would you? Well, here are a couple of pretty good ones right here—me and you."

"What are you going to do? I didn't mean to jump you. I thought it was a guard coming." The man struggled to sit up now.

ARTHUR hesitated in pity for the fear-sick creature. But how could he hamper his own flight with this one? Yet if he left, the Syn the euthanasia chamber would soon accommodate him.

He wondered how the Syn had broken loose. Then he saw the grotesquely twisted body of the attendant lying in a heap on the floor behind the door. The merchant must have jumped him as the careless attendant unmanacled him. A ring of manual keys was on the floor, but ordinarily the locks were opened by electrical controls, which Arthur had watched the doctor operate to free this door for him.

Arthur grinned. "Most Syns must be so dispirited that they don't put up much fight or this fellow would have been more careful. You did a good job on him."

"What are we going to do?" the merchant repeated. "I couldn't make them understand that I'm not a Syn. They won't listen to me."

"Don't you think it was this way with all the others who have gone through here? Don't you think they felt the same?"

"No—they were all Syns. They knew they had it coming—"

"How about me? Have I got it coming, too?"

The Syn's eyes widened in a new fear as if the thought had not occurred to him that he was putting Arthur on the other side from himself.

"It's a good joke, isn't it?" said Arthur. "I'm going to get away, and they're going to put one of their own kind in the chamber. Funny, isn't it?"

He understood fully, now. The Syns *didn't* know their own identity beforehand—and not knowing, they shared the common brutality of mankind.

"Take me with you," The Syn whimpered. "We can find the Syn underground organization. It's big. Tell them I'm one of you and let me live with you among them."

"You said that Syns and men could not live together."

"Please—we've got to hurry. They'll find us out here."

"But you would not give a single Syn the mercy you are grasping, would you?"

"Please…"

"All right, come on. Let's get out of here."

They went down the long passage without interference, nor did Arthur expect any. CS had prepared the way. It was when they were outside that there would be trouble.

They found the car at the end of the corridor, as had been promised. "We'll take this," said Arthur.

His companion got in without speaking, his fat body trembling in every contour. His brow was beaded with perspiration.

Arthur warmed the motor for a few seconds, then gunned it heavily and snapped into the main driveway with a snarl of the wheels. Without a single glance at the guardpost, he burst through the open gates and into the street.

Then from the buildings behind them there came the long low wail of siren warnings, the dread notification of escaped Syns at large in the city.

Arthur wheeled the fast, heavy car through the dark and silent streets toward Old Town. From far behind came the sound of sirens on CS cars plunging in pursuit. Ahead, he saw the ruins of Old Town dimly silhouetted against the starry sky.

THE NIGHT seemed to become darker as he found the poverty-ridden streets bordering Old Town. He cruised down the alleys at the rear of the ancient houses that lined them. On the car he reduced the head beams to a narrow pencil of light.

"Down there!" suddenly exclaimed his companion. He was pointing off towards the darkest, most dismal alley they had seen. "Let's try to hide down that one."

It looked as good as any to Arthur. He wheeled the car into the narrow, debris-lined drive, but they could never make contact with the Syns in the car, he thought. They would have to abandon it, but how could he get rid of it without exciting the suspicions of his companion?

He took the only obvious way. As if by accident, he drove at a fast clip into the long row of weathered fencing that lined the alley. The fat Syn screamed as he saw the shattered boards flying through the air and crashing about them.

The terrible crunching died away as all sense of motion vanished. Then they heard the crackle of flames in the dry wreckage.

Arthur dragged the whimpering fat man from the broken car and stood him on his feet, slapping his face vigorously.

"Come on! They'll have the whole block surrounded in a minute."

The distant sirens were nearing, and already they had roused the sleeping neighborhood. Night terror for these people had been replaced by the hope of vengeance upon some of those responsible for their misery.

There were sudden cries from windows on every side as they ran down the alley in the glare of the rising flames: "Syns! There they go! Don't let them get away!"

The fat Syn was soon puffing heavily, and the sound of other running feet was plainly heard behind them now. The mob was gathering, and Arthur knew he would have to abandon the fat man to them if he couldn't keep up.

They crossed the street at the end of the alley. Arthur hesitated for an instant to decide whether to turn or to continue along the alley. Blindly, the frightened Syn plunged on ahead. Arthur followed. It was as good a way as any.

He caught up quickly, cursing the stumbling steps and sobbing breath of the Syn.

"Come on, damn you," he snarled. "They'll have us like a pack of wolves if they ever catch up with us."

"What good is it?" The Syn sobbed. "Where can we go? How, can we hide?"

In sudden renewal of pity, Arthur realized the hapless Syn was only fleeing blindly without goal or plan in mind. He tried to put himself in the Syn's place, running from certain death. It was impossible, because he had no such hazard. Capture that meant only another freedom for him was sure death for the Syn.

He stopped and patted the soft flabby arm of the merchant. "We'll find our way out of this, I promise you that."

He didn't stop to analyze the utter foolishness of this rash promise. He only looked frantically ahead into the darkness, hoping for the sight of a beckoning Syn who might offer them refuge and safety. From behind, the mob sounds increased.

Abruptly, a tube of light thrust down through the darkness from far behind, bathing them in a brilliant flow of illumination. At once the cries increased to a howling fury. Arthur looked back. It was a spotlight mounted on one of the CS cars that was trying to force itself down through the mob choking the alley.

The crazy fools! They didn't have to make it so realistic, Arthur thought. In that light it would be almost impossible for a Syn emissary to reach them and lead them out of the way. He suspected Trask and Benson had given orders that punches were not to be pulled in any degree whatever.

HE RESUMED flight, dragging the despairing Syn by one arm. With a moan of anguish, the Syn jerked back, pointing to the opposite end of the alley that was now visible in the light of the CS beam.

The alley ended abruptly in a board wall.

The CS car was at the head of the mob now a scant hundred yards behind them. The officers could pick up their quarry at will. Any holding back by them would betray the purpose of this make-believe flight.

It was a stupid thing to have run into a dead end alley, but even if they hadn't done so Arthur wondered just how escape might have been possible. He felt a deep respect for those Syns who had achieved freedom in such pursuit as this. Ardyth, he thought, had succeeded.

But suppose he *was* a Syn? He wouldn't be giving up even now. He would be driving every neuron of his brain to produce an answer, a way out of this dead-end alley.

It made a difference. Self-preservation instincts were active in his Syn companion even though failing Arthur. "There's trash at the end," said the Syn. "Maybe we can scale the fence."

"Right. Let's make it to the end as fast as we can go."

They slammed their bodies into the fence and hung gasping as if impaled by the force of their momentum. Like some terrible piston thrusting along the cylinder in which they were trapped, the mob with the CS car at its head was driving down the narrow alley.

The Syn moved towards the trash pile and began struggling to the top of it in the full glare of the light. He reached for the top of a stack of crates to hoist himself up. Slowly, the pile arced back under the impetus of his weight. He screamed in panic as the pile tilted and fell, his cries becoming lost in the rumble of collapsing boxes and shattering crates.

Arthur leaped to tear the pile of material from on top of his companion. He could hear the individual cries of the mob where there had been only a mass of indistinguishable sound before.

"Don't let them get away! Kill the dirty Syns! Get behind the fence—don't let them get over it—"

"Stand still and raise your hands or we'll shoot!" This was a cry in which Arthur recognized the authority of the CS voice. But he continued his task of rousing the fallen Syn.

"Get up!" he demanded fiercely. "Get up or I'll leave you there."

He didn't know if the Syn was hurt or not; there was no chance of examination now. Then, as he straightened from shifting the debris, he noticed the thin, dark line of a gate in the high fence, a gate revealed by the collapse of the pile of debris.

The Syn stood, shaken, and looked into the glare of the lights.

"We're lost!" he moaned.

"There's a gate right here behind the trash," Arthur said. "Can't tell if it's locked or not, but let's rush it to-gether. They'll fire as we move, but one of us may make it."

They moved as one man, scrambling over the pile of trash, then down behind the peak of it. Their bodies smashed into the gate. It remained, a solid immovable part of the fence.

THEIR SWIFT rush signaled the crash of bullets, thundering in the alley. Splinters whined as they twisted through the air. Arthur dragged the Syn down, hiding partly between the fence and the trash pile.

Then from somewhere that seemed almost beside them they heard a new and unbelievable sound—the answering thunder of gunfire directed towards the mob.

Arthur raised his head in careless amazement. From a narrow crack between the boards he saw another burst of fire. Then a voice snarled huskily at them, "Get down, you fools. We'll have this gate open in a minute—there. Come on through!"

There was screaming in the alley. Someone had been hit by those defending bullets. Now the mob was firing on its own. Arthur heard the cursing cries of the CS men trying to halt the angered group, threatening to fire into them. But the officers were helpless now, and Arthur understood they would not fire into the mob to save even him. They couldn't without risking their own lives. This was what Trask had warned against.

Bullets crashed close as he fell through the open gate with his Syn companion. Hands reached for them in the darkness beyond the fence. Firm hands clutched each arm and led them swiftly away towards the dark buildings nearby.

"The mob will be over that fence in a few seconds!" Arthur warned. "We've got to get away from here."

"Let us take care of that," said the stranger at his left.

They hurried into the darkest shadows as the first wave of the mob broke over the fence and crashed through the gate, choking it with their own bodies.

Then, in the half darkness of the scene, Arthur saw two shadowy figures dart away from the mob. The cries of rage funneled in their direction and swift pursuit was renewed. He understood then. Two skilled Syns were acting as decoys for himself and his companion to lead the mob away while they were guided to safety.

The four who had rescued him watched in silent satisfaction, then one turned in the darkness and spoke. "We welcome you, fellow Syns. Welcome to the brotherhood of outcast humanity!"

CHAPTER SIX

IN THE distance on one hand the sounds of the mob died, and on the other the crackle of flames was subdued by the hiss of foam clouds. Silent darkness settled over the sick and weary city once again.

At the side of the building the Syns opened a cellar door leading into the depths beneath. Without lights, they moved by sense of perception only. An increasing smell of mustiness became nearly stifling. After a time they halted, the guides fumbling with some hidden door catch in the darkness.

Then, as a portal opened, the party passed through and the door slammed behind them as if with a heavy seal, shutting out all sound, engulfing them in silence that bore the illusion of utter sanctuary. The lights came on with blinding suddenness.

"Welcome to the country and possessions of the Syns."

Arthur turned to the guide who spoke. He might have been a lithe and muscular man once, but his face was bleached a sickly color now is if he had lived in this warren away from the sun for a long time.

They were all like that. Their faces and bodies bore the marks of hiding and living with the constant fear of pursuit and death.

"We've forgotten the names we once had," the Syn guide said, "just as we've had to forget we once were humans. Lack of identification has some precautionary features, which is the main reason for its adoption. I am known as James. These men are Clark, Wallace, and Barkley. You may introduce yourself by any term you choose, and it will be that by which you are known for the rest of your life among us."

Arthur saw no good reason for assuming a pseudonym. "I am Arthur," he said.

"Good enough, and you—?" He turned to the fat merchant who hesitated as if suddenly intrigued by the necessity of framing a mask to hide him all the rest of his days, a mask that had to be a golden, magnificent thing to counterbalance the shoddy, unbelievable fate that had befallen him.

"Laurence," he said with exaggerated motions of his mouth and lips as if savoring some delicacy. "I like Laurence. I shall be Laurence."

Even the four Syns smiled at this feeble attempt of the merchant to elevate himself with a name.

"Laurence it shall be," said James. "Make yourselves comfortable, gentlemen. You will rest a day or two here. I suppose you haven't eaten—?"

There was a small and ancient freezer well stocked with food, and canned goods were stacked on shelves. Arthur wondered about their source of supplies and activities that were directed from this location. He wondered about Ardyth, and how much closer he was to her because of this step. But those questions would have to wait for later answers.

He sank down on one of the ill-kept beds and closed his eyes. He let the reaction come now, the reaction of understanding how close he had been to death in that alley trap. There was something he didn't like about that. The fact was not in the probability that Eddie had given. The logic engine had not indicated danger at this point, though Trask and Benson had warned of it.

In dismay, he suddenly recognized that if Ardyth had adopted a pseudonym somewhere in the warrens of the Syns she was still as remote as ever.

He sat up sharply.

"What happens next?" he demanded. "Where do we go from here?"

CLARK SPOKE up from beside the tiny, radiant stove where he cooked, "Go? You don't go anywhere from here. This is the end of the world, didn't you know?"

James rose from his own bed across the room. He smiled without humor and came over to put a hand on Arthur's shoulder. On the way, he patted Clark's back affectionately.

"Don't let Clark get you down with that. We've got better plans than that, but he's only been here a couple of months. The rest of us have been here over a year—old timers."

They were young, Arthur discovered with a kind of shock. James had thick black hair that once had been well cared for. He'd been a good-looking guy before this. All of them, except for their unnatural pallor, could have passed for ordinary, competent young engineers or technicians, young husbands and fathers of normal society.

"We're as human as the rest of the world," said James savagely. "Don't ever forget that. Just because they've kicked us out doesn't mean that we're robot monsters.

We're men! Get that into your skull and don't ever let it out. The classification as Syns changes nothing of your actual nature. You're exactly what you were before you acquired a new name. You're a man, understand?"

"No. If I'm a thing made by a machine I am not a man and never can be."

"You can go crazy—just like a man—and that's what will happen if you keep on thinking like that. Listen, we're everything that men ever were and a lot more besides. Think of that crazy, howling mob out there that nearly murdered you. Would you be glad to be one of *them?*

"Syns are more than men. We're the new inheritors of Earth. Look at the mess that men have made of Earth ever since they have possessed it. They're born and bred and live out their miserable lives tottering on the very edge of insanity, and half of them dip over during a good part of their lives.

"The Syns can never do that. We're sane. We're whole. We're what men might have become and never did. And we'll replace men in the end, and make something of this world that they've torn up with their wars.

"You needn't be ashamed. You can be proud you are a Syn. You shall inherit the Earth…"

James' voice had risen and his jaw muscles stood out in knots at the side of his face. His eyes burned with fierce conviction.

Arthur watched him, his eyes searching the finely shaped skull, the pallid skin through which forehead veins pulsed feverishly. This was something that Arthur had not dreamed of. He had pictured the Syns as beaten dregs of life that had once passed for human. In James he seemed to be witnessing the resurrection of a man.

"How will that come about?" he said quietly. "Will we be forced to resort to the same force that you have branded as insanity in men?"

"We may. We hope not. In the end, we'll simply out-number men. Then all killing will stop. We'll give men a piece of the Earth to live on, and show them how to live if they'll listen. If they won't, we'll let them die out through lack of breeding. But whatever men do, the world belongs now to the Syns."

THE SIX of them moved to sit about the table as Clark finished setting out the food. Laurence seemed suddenly as pale as if he'd remembered some long forgotten ghost.

"My family might be sitting down to dinner now," he said in a muted voice. "They won't know about me, will they? They won't know at all—"

He looked at the circle about him, his moon face warping with grief.

"Let it come, fellow," said James quietly. "We all went through it. Lie down on the bed there if you don't feel like eating anything."

Arthur covered the awkwardness of Laurence's weeping. "How can the Syns increase their numbers under present condition? It seems more likely to me that we'll be exterminated."

"We're working night and day to find the reproduction centers," said James. "When we do we'll be able to control them and guide all new Syns to us, where they can be protected until they develop."

"You mean you don't know the locations of the machines that produced us!" exclaimed Arthur. "Are there no Syns who have memory of their connection with the machine?"

"Barkley claims a kind of recollection, but he can't be sure. None of the rest of us have any. Rather, most of us remember families and parents, just like anyone else. That's because the machine put those memories into us so that we could pass as conventional humans without betraying our origin. Everything would have gone as the machine originally planned if that damned logic engine hadn't discovered this one betraying feature that the encephalograph reveals."

"Haven't you been able to test these memories by contact with parents, for example, after being declared a Syn?"

"Wallace, you tell the man about that."

The black eyes of Wallace were deep in his cavernous face and roily with bitterness. "I tested it," he said. "I went back to my parents' house after I was told I was a suspected Syn. They told the CS men they had never seen me before. They threw me out to be killed without a word of recognition or sympathy."

"You can't blame those people!" exclaimed James. "It was true they had never seen you before. The machine had given you memories of parents like them so you assumed you were their son. It must have terrified them to have a total stranger walking up claiming to be their son—and a Syn, at that. They aren't to blame."

"I don't know," said Wallace wearily. "I just don't know any more. But I do know that we have to push on as if we did know all the answers. I've got to believe in the machine, and in the Syns. There's no man in whom I can believe any longer."

"We're going to locate those machines. Maybe Syns in other parts of the world have already done so. One major problem is establishing communication with such groups. We are handicapped in that, you can understand."

"Before I left Earth for Cyprian II where I spent the last couple of years," said Arthur—slowly, "I was engaged to marry a girl. While I was gone, she was found to be a Syn and escaped. My first objective is to find her—if she is still alive. Here is her picture. Her name was Ardyth, if she has not changed it. Have any of you ever seen her?"

He passed the photo around the table and it came to rest in front of James. The big, tense man seemed to go a shade more pallid, and Clark gave a sudden snort.

"Know her? We haven't heard of anything else for weeks. James has the idea that she has promised to marry *him!*"

CHAPTER SEVEN

THEY REMAINED within the warren the following day. At nightfall, James planned to take them to the Syn's central headquarters. They ate light meals, mostly from force of habit, for all hunger except that for freedom and companionship had left them.

James' attitude throughout the day was perceptibly colder, but at times he tried to make up for it with spasmodic over-demonstrations of friendliness. Arthur liked the Syn group leader in spite of his fantastic claim to Ardyth.

He was not afraid of any possible validity to that claim, but Ardyth's treatment the past year might have thrown her into such despair that she had abandoned the dreams she and Arthur had known, and had sought refuge in such love as James offered her.

He felt sorry, too, for he sensed that James' love for her was real, and his burden of bitterness would be doubled when she had to renounce him. He almost hoped their two Ardyths were not the same. But James said there was no doubt of the identity, and promised to take Arthur to her.

As evening approached, a sense of urgency and expectancy began to grow in the movements of the four Syns who understood what was ahead of them at this time.

"I want to now show you our communication system," James told Arthur. "It's about time for our scheduled roll call."

He took Arthur to a small adjacent room which none of them had entered during the day. Within it was a broad table covered with a litter of crude but ingenious-looking equipment. James sat down at the chair before the table.

"The city is ringed by such posts as ours. Communication is by infrared beams. Each post is in line of sight with at least two others. These eyepieces will give you a look at the two others adjacent to us."

Arthur bent down to peer through. Along a very narrow and precarious line of sight, he saw distant, unobtrusive buildings like the one that covered their warren. One seemed about a mile away, and the other somewhat less.

"An automatic alarm rings when either line of sight is accidentally or purposely obstructed," said James. "It is our only source of communication. In just a moment our turn for roll call will come."

Even as he spoke, a small light began flashing on the table. He put on a set of phones and listened carefully, then began tapping an ancient telegraph key.

The contact finished, he laid down the phones and glanced up speculatively at Arthur. "It seems your fame has spread already. We reported your arrival in routine contact last night. The First Created has a detailed re-port on you and orders your appearance tonight. Special guard arrangements are being made for your safety. You must have something the First wants pretty badly."

"The First Created—who is he?" said Arthur. "You haven't mentioned him before. And how did he get such a report on me?"

James smiled. "There's a lot that I haven't mentioned, but you'll find out gradually. The First is our leader. He was the first one created by the machines, and we have him to thank for the organization and relative security that we enjoy. He was especially endowed by the creating machine with many qualities that the rest of us lack."

"But even he does not know where the machines are located?"

"No. He has assigned that to all of us as our prime goal."

During the day, James had prepared counterfeit test cards for Arthur and Laurence. These, he turned over to them now.

WHEN IT was too dark for observation without lights, but not late enough to be conspicuous, they left the warren. Arthur discovered then that the upper quarters, the house itself, were occupied by an old lady who kept "roomers." A Syn, she fronted for the warren. Similar setups camouflaged the other posts about the city.

They left in two groups of three. James and Clark went with Arthur in the first car. Many minutes later the other three departed in an entirely separate direction.

For the first time, Arthur was seeing the city as one of the ostracized. He sensed how high and how strong was the wall that separated the Syns from mankind. There was terror in it that made him want to rush out and frantically proclaim his humanity.

Then he looked askance at his companions and knew that he could never fully comprehend their feelings for they could not be moved to such a proclamation. They knew they were not of the substance of mankind.

In the busiest part of town Clark took the car on alone. Arthur and James went into a public restaurant and ordered a meal that offered more substance than the cooking in the warren, which was emergency type only.

The division of the party was perhaps necessary camouflage, Arthur thought, and their coming here was part of a desperate yearning to believe that men were once more kindly creatures who could be trusted and made friends with.

As they ate, Arthur glanced about. People talked but little or not at all. Most were alone at single tables, eyes concentrating on their food in desperate intensity as if afraid of unseen enemies who might seize them momentarily.

Suddenly the heads of the diners raised as if at news of some reprieve. Their eyes gradually lighted with bestial anticipation.

Arthur turned to the direction of their gaze. In the street a knot of people was swiftly growing to a writhing mob that blocked all traffic on street and walks. Its nucleus could not be discerned fully, but the top of a car showed in the center of the mob.

"What—?" Arthur began, and then he understood by the expression on the faces of the mob. He had to eat while murder took place before his eyes.

The diners were rising and rushing to the window in gleeful expectancy. One flabby, well-dressed man stopped at their table in breathless excitement. "Come on!" he invited. "Looks like they've caught another one of those lousy Syns out there. Don't you want to watch it?"

"No thanks," said Arthur easily. "We have an appointment we must meet—have to finish up here so that we can be on our way."

James had stopped eating, his face bloodless with panic. For the first time Arthur realized how close the Syn was to cracking up. Long months of hovering death had put a thin edge to his resistance. The Syns were not the strong men they claimed, he thought. The ostracism and the constant threat of death was as heavy a burden to them as it would have been to a man.

OUTSIDE, the sound was like that at some magnificent sporting event. This was the way it must have sounded in the Coliseum of ancient Rome. This is the way it must have been while Joan of Arc burned, and while the witches of old Salem died.

He felt as if the food inside him was being loaded onto a catapult, but he warned the Syn sharply. "Start eating!"

James nodded with even greater understanding than Arthur possessed. "I've seen mobs in a mood like this grab up anyone who looked as if he disapproved in the slightest degree."

Some of the color returned to his face as if the panic had come under control. "We can slip out the side door facing the other street when we're through," he said.

Arthur tried to keep his eyes and thoughts on his food, but he kept hearing the obscene sounds from both the street and his fellow diners who crowded the windows. Then he heard the other sounds that were the cries of the attacked, the sound of human despair.

"I'm not a Syn——! Won't somebody believe me? I tell you they made a mistake——!"

James stiffened, half rising in his chair.

"Easy, you fool…"

"That voice—it's——"

"Yes, but tell me what we can do about it."

"Nothing—nothing——"

The top of the car had seemed vaguely familiar, Arthur thought. As James sank slowly to the chair again, they both imagined the three Syns out there—Barkley and Wallace, and frightened, fat little Laurence who had chosen a brave name to cover the fear that was in him.

Arthur wondered how on Earth they had been spotted—and if they, then why not he and James?

Breaking glass tinkled through the screams. It was a brutal miracle that on such a barren street so many rocks could be found so quickly. Then there was the sudden flash of yellow flame and the odor of burning oil.

The mob uttered its own cries of warning and backed from the billowing flames. Heat forced them even from the window and then Arthur could see his companions of those brief night hours.

Wallace was slumped over the seat of the car, his face almost beyond recognition with the work of the stoning. On the street, Laurence was huddled, his squat body like a small tent billowed out to full expanse. His head rolled back and forth while vain prayers for mercy gorged from his throat.

Barkley was still upright and fighting back. Reaching for the stones as swiftly as they came, he had already forced back a small segment of the mob with his fury.

Illustration by Rod Ruth

Although the heat from the burning car had driven them far back from it, he stood as if unnoticing, and Arthur heard the awed whisper of a man by the window.

"Look at it! A man couldn't stand that, but he doesn't even notice it. You'd almost think we could have made some use of them."

"We could—if they didn't think they were as good as men. But I wouldn't want to run the risk of having a single one of them loose. When we get them cleaned out, I'll be the first to suggest lynching anyone who dares proposing that any be retained for any purpose."

"Yeah—I guess you're right."

BARKLEY HAD fallen now and the bulge he had driven in the mob quickly filled and curved towards him, seeking revenge for his temporary triumph. His head was

crushed and bleeding, but slowly he struggled to his feet, his face almost obliterated.

Slow curses of awe were murmured by the watchers at the window. "If men only had guts like that—"

"But it's not a man. Nothing but a damned machine. That isn't guts—it's only lack of feeling. Sure does look real, though, doesn't it? Blood and everything—"

The hand of Barkley passed slowly across the bloody face, and in that mangled contour Arthur saw—or imagined he saw—a face of deep peace that he had never seen upon a man.

More than men, James had said. Was it true? Were these the successors to mankind in their inheritance of the Earth?

The figure of Barkley collapsed suddenly before the onslaught of stones and fire, and Arthur thought of other causes that had risen Phoenix-like from martyrs' ashes. Barkley's fall was not the fall of merely a Syn. It was, perhaps, the fall of all mankind.

With leisurely disinterest, Arthur rose from the table. Together, he and James strode towards the counter. The sickness eating within James had retreated enough so that he smiled at the cashier. "Do we pay extra for the show?" he inquired.

But it was lost upon her. Already she was sinking back into the dread uncertainty of the coming night in which no man would know his neighbor, and the fearful witch-hunt would go on.

She accepted his money and they walked out as the diners who had watched by the windows returned to their cold plates. Outside, the thick vapor of oil smoke hung low in the street and carried with it the stench of burned flesh.

"Which way?" said Arthur.

"To the right. Clark should pick us up along the street here somewhere."

The car in which they had left the warren slid to a stop beside them almost before he was aware of it. Clark's face was haggard and wild with suspicion of pursuit.

They climbed in beside him, and he drove off with a cavalier wheeling of the car.

"Take it slower," cautioned James. "You saw back there?"

"Yes. I was almost even with them when it happened. It was horrible. Thank Heaven I'm not a human. They are monsters that ought to be wiped off the Earth. It will be easy enough for me to take part in any extermination of them."

"But you had seen the same thing before—from the other side—"

Clark nodded slowly. "Yes. Once I even laughed when I saw a Syn dying. I thought he was no more than a grotesque, mechanical thing."

"If that's the way *they* felt then perhaps we can't blame them too much."

"Oh, I don't know... How is it possible to see both sides—to have been on both of them without becoming insane?"

Clark was right, thought Arthur, and he had forgotten until now the vicious pleasure of Laurence anticipating that Arthur might be shown up as a Syn.

It made no sense. They were all swabbed with the same black brush, men and Syns—until the separation came that proved one to be a man and the other a thing of artifice.

He was sure he did not have the whole picture yet. Elements were lacking that had to be fitted in to give reason and coherency to the insane puzzle.

"How were they spotted?" James asked. "I thought we were covered perfectly."

"It was one of those things that wouldn't happen in a thousand years. The euthanasia guard Laurence slugged was passing on the street and recognized Laurence in the car. He screamed the word Syn, and that was it.

"The crowd bared their fangs and started drooling for blood. I don't see why we are almost like them before we are separated out, and why we can't do our own separating before they try us for our lives."

James ignored the question that Clark placed. Instead, he pointed ahead to the mass of buildings that rose at the end of the street.

"This is it."

ARTHUR stared ahead. The structures were those of the Exner Construction Company, interstellar engineers. It was they who had built the basic structures into which Arthur had assembled the automatic machines for the factories of the Cyprians.

"How can you meet here?" he exclaimed. "How can you keep a thing like this secret in the middle of a great plant like Exner?"

"We don't have to." James smiled with faint humor. "The entire Exner Company is the nucleus of the Syn organization."

"But I've worked with their engineers!"

"Then you have worked with Syns. Dr. Exner himself is the First Created."

"I've seen him from a distance only, but I know his men consider him a first-rate genius."

"He is, and you'll soon find it out for yourself."

Clark drove the car through the heavy steel gates, flashing a signal at a watchman who admitted them. They came to a stop near the large, four-story administration and design building.

Arthur followed his companions up the somewhat familiar stairway and corridors. He tried hastily to recall what he knew of Dr. Exner. The man had once worked for Allied. He had worked on the design of Eddie during the first planning of the logic engine, and he had been called in for work and consultation during the time Arthur was on Cyprian.

Exner had always remained uncommunicative and reserved. He made few friends among the staff at Allied, but no one ever doubted his ability or his genius.

For Arthur, however, it was utterly impossible to imagine him in the position of Syn leadership, for him to be the mystic so-called First Created.

James stopped abruptly before a broad door of grandly polished wood. He pressed a small case against an unobtrusive panel near the center of it. The door swung inward, and they were in the presence of Dr. Exner. First Created of all the Syns.

CHAPTER EIGHT

HE WAS looking up at them from behind the massive desk that was covered with a few neatly arranged papers. He had the same unhealthy pallor that Arthur had come to think as the hallmark of the Syns. It was almost a grayish tinge that matched the close-cropped hair. The lines of his bullet-shaped head were revealed with unattractive clarity, and the grayness of his hair seemed distinguishable from the grayness of his face only by the textural quality of each.

"I am happy to see you, Arthur Zoran," he said slowly. "I had long hoped that your return to Earth would find you in our midst. The Syns have great need of your talents.

"You have done very well, James and Clark. Please leave us now, and I will continue the instructions you have so well begun."

The shadow of hostility, absent the past hours, fell again over the face of James, but his smile belied it. "I'll be seeing you," he said. He left with Clark in tow.

"Sit down, please," said Dr. Exner. "I am sure that James has answered many of your preliminary questions; but if there is anything in particular that you want to know, I'll try to answer it for you."

"There's only one thing I want to know: The whereabouts of my fiancée, Ardyth Crane. James claims to know her—that she has promised to marry him. I want to see her."

"There is an Ardyth here—one of our most excellent and valued workers."

Arthur flashed the small plastic picture across the desk. Dr. Exner glanced at it briefly and nodded. "She is the one of whom James spoke. I will take you to her as soon as we are through here."

Take me to her, now, you damned old fool! Arthur thought fiercely.

But there was no way on Earth to force the impassive mask that faced him across the desk. The whites of Exner's eyes seemed curiously large and alive almost as if with a light of their own. It gave his whole face an expression of high, fanatic purpose, in which the destiny of any human—or any Syn—was of small consequence.

He was silent for a long moment, and then he began speaking in a voice so low that for a moment Arthur wondered if he had missed the first few words.

"We are the future race of mankind," said Exner. "We are the super race of which idealists have dreamed down through the ages. The destiny of Earth is in our hands."

"But we have to find first who made us, and how," said Arthur. "That is what James told me."

"He is correct. That is our immediate goal, and I think you will be able to help us find the answer—you and our mutual friend, Eddie."

"Eddie…"

"Yes. I think Eddie knows where the machines are."

Arthur thought swiftly back to that night when Eddie had denied such knowledge. Almost he forgot his double role to blurt out the fact of his previous questioning of Eddie and the denial.

"You will be interested—and perhaps amazed—to learn how I first came to know of our inheritance," said Exner. "The logic engine was directly responsible for it."

"How was that possible?"

"It was when I first planned the organization of my own company. I was nearing the end of my contract with Allied and wanted to get an engine analysis on my plans. Since this was forbidden, of course, I secretly used the machine one night on the pretense of necessary repairs to it.

"During the course of feeding in my personal data, the question of time came up, time which might be available to me to build up the kind of organization I envisioned. As I proceeded I kept getting the most absurd answers with respect to time. Finally, I put the question directly as to why such answers were given. Eddie replied that they were not meaningless and asked if I did not know that I was virtually immortal—that I had at least ten life spans in which I might plan and proceed with my work."

"The Syns have such a life span?" Arthur exclaimed.

DR. EXNER nodded as if trying to convey the magnitude of that discovery as he had felt it on that night.

"Then the engine almost expressed amazement that I had not deduced the logical fact of my artificial creation from the factors I had given it. Eddie went on to describe in great detail how Syns originate in one of the automatic chemical research plants in exactly the same way that all life originated in the primal chemical vat of the sea."

"It's an almost impossible thing to believe," said Arthur. "Is there no other evidence except the story of the logic engine? Couldn't he tell more of this plant that did the work? And how can we be sure he did not withhold something of importance?"

"You're an engineer on logic engines. You know the safeguards against error. Besides, I put the data into him again and again. All through the night I checked and got the same answers.

"But in one respect I believe you are correct in your questioning. I think information has been held back— but only because the question has not been properly asked by one capable of understanding the answer. You are the one I consider able to ask the question and receive that answer."

"I don't know—perhaps—"

Arthur was imagining such a night as Dr. Exner had once known. He felt a sympathy for the lonely man who had been the first to suddenly learn he was not of human kind.

"What did you do when you found this out?" he asked.

"What would any ordinary man have done? I expected to get married soon. How could I—a thing that was not even a man? I made careful checks. The memory that I had was one implanted by the machine. Nothing of the things I remembered could be checked with reality very closely. Parents were dead in the War, of course. I told the girl I was to marry that I could not go through with it. I broke her heart as well as my own.

"Then gradually I began to see the importance of the knowledge I had been given. It was something that went far beyond my own petty welfare. It concerned the whole world of men and Syns, for I was the only one of either who knew of the existence of a division between them."

"Didn't Eddie reveal the knowledge to others?"

"I cautioned against it, and introduced factors into the circuits to prevent it, but I knew that they would be removed sooner or later. There was no logic in my desired suppression, so I knew that it would eventually come out. I was hardly prepared for the way in which it was revealed."

"How was that?"

"You should know, first, what I did to prepare the way for other Syns. Eddie gave the electroencephalograph test to me and I used it to build up this company of Syns. Not one of us had an inkling of our identity before the test revealed it. I made the tests during occupational interviews.

"The War wiped out most family connections of the present generation so that, in general, family remembrances were impossible to check. In some instances there was conflicting information. Parents seemed to have a definite knowledge of the birth of their child, who was a Syn. Some of this data has not yet been adequately accounted for, chiefly because all our work has had to be concealed.

"We were a bewildered, half-embittered lot, aware of our own bastard inheritance and not knowing exactly what to do with it. We laid plans to find the centers of reproduction that had turned us into the stream of humanity to take the part of men. This remains our greatest task.

"Then, overnight, everything changed for us. Eddie revealed to an Allied technician while you were gone that he was also a Syn and explained the significance, evidently in response to forbidden questioning of the kind I had done. The knowledge broke the mind of the creature, and when he was examined the whole story got out. Then the horror of extermination began.

"We quickly prepared counterfeit defenses for ourselves. We learned to modify our brainwaves to pass the tests, but we could do nothing except watch while thousands of our fellow Syns were slaughtered. We had no way of locating them *first*.

"But along with horror came a purpose to our existence. We saw the many ways in which we are superior to men. We watched the insanity of the witch-hunt spread to the whole world, and we understood our destiny.

"We are ready now to take what is our own. And do not believe that we come with a gospel of peace. Ours is as bloody as men's. The post you were taken to was no mere warren. It is an arsenal, a fort. A score of them ring the entire city, and they mount weapons whose force can make it all ours within short hours. Ten thousand trained Syns wait night and day for my command to take what is rightfully ours.

"I want no peace. I want Syns to hate humans forever, and someday there will be no humans at all, and Syns shall inherit the Earth and make of it the garden it was meant to be. And you—you shall help us, though your miserable, short life will hardly make it possible for you to take part in the enjoyment of our paradise!"

DR. EXNER'S face split abruptly in a thin smile of inexplicable intent. Arthur leaned forward as if by close scrutiny he could read the hidden meaning momentarily revealed.

"What do you mean by that...?" he demanded softly.

Exner's face relapsed quickly into a gray mask again. The overhead lights cast a curtain of shadow over his cheeks and his eyes were like great pools of porcelain through which the tiny pupils looked with omniscient glare.

"I mean," he said, "that your little play has fooled no one. You had not a chance in the world of making your way into our organization by playing that you were a Syn. You were watched and led along the entire way."

Arthur felt as if the base of his tongue were suddenly swollen too large for his throat. His words seemed harsh as they came from his dry mouth.

"I don't understand—I don't understand what you mean—"

"Of course you do. We are not fools. Do you think we could have existed this long if we had no better safeguards against intrusion than you have supposed?

"We know that you are a human. We know that you came to spy on us, hoping to determine the source of our reproduction in order to destroy us. We know that is your job."

"How do you know that?"

"Trask and Benson gave us the first word that you were coming. They are both Syns. So, likewise, is the doctor at the examination center who passed you through. As you may guess, he frees the most valuable of the Syns and sends as many humans to their deaths. We like the irony of that.

"And then your little companion, Laurence, was placed to spot you and lead you. Do you understand?"

With shameful hindsight, Arthur recalled now the offhand way the fat merchant had suggested the alley down which they should go, how he had been the one to reveal the gate in the fence by tearing down the trash pile—

"If all this supposition is true, what happens next? You didn't let me come here just to be killed. That much is obvious."

"No. We let you come—we wanted you to come—because we need you. We planned to obtain your help in any manner possible, but Eddie solved that problem very nicely by sending you to us.

"We need access to the logic engine. You are our only contact that is competent to handle it. Doc Trainer is also one of us, and we had high hopes when he was appointed to fill your place—but he has failed to get the information we need.

"Then I proposed this plan. You will be sent back to Allied, reporting tentative failure, but will keep on trying to accomplish your original purpose. You will report to *us* through the CS men, what you learn of our origin from Eddie. Trask and Benson, incidentally, will shoot without warning if you attempt betrayal. They are authorized as CS humans to kill on their own initiative, and it would cause little concern in these days of nervous minds and quick killing."

"Why did you go through all the shadow play of my coming here through my own plan? Why wasn't I simply kidnapped?"

"That would have destroyed much of your usefulness. As it is, you have a legitimate relationship with both our group and your own. You will proceed to find the answer—just as both groups desire. But you will report only to us…"

"And what makes you think I will do all this quite willingly, and without, perhaps, selecting my own death as the alternative?"

"Why?" Dr. Exner suddenly assumed a somewhat astounded expression. "Have I underestimated your talents after all?"

"I am asking," Arthur repeated evenly.

"We have Ardyth! You will do anything we ask as long as she is in our hands."

"She is a Syn, you told me," Arthur replied. He tried to keep his voice from registering the blow that Exner had delivered.

"So she is," Exner chuckled. "A Syn, a composition of inert atoms put together by a purposeless machine. She is nothing but a machine herself, just like the rest of us. I could destroy her, molecule by molecule, atom by atom, and listen to her screams until she died, and it would mean nothing whatever for I am also a Syn and I know that the thing that you humans call emotion has no existence or meaning for us.

"But you—you are a man, and you love Ardyth. No rationalization of which your mind is capable will ever convince you she is a mechanical creation, an emotionless thing of mere chemicals that possessed no soul. No, as long as you live, and she exists, she will be Ardyth, the girl you love, and you will not do anything at all that might result in harm to her. Is that not so?"

"You devil...you inhuman devil..." Arthur murmured through pale lips.

Dr. Exner laughed uproariously. "You see? I *am* right!"

CHAPTER NINE

HE SAW ARDYTH through the open doorway of a small room that looked out upon the broad expanse of the Exner property grounds. She was sitting quietly at a desk, and the light beside her made a golden cloud of her hair.

Dr. Exner urged him forward with a touch on his arm. "Go on in. She objected strongly to my plan, but she knows you're coming."

Arthur strode in, slamming the door behind him.

Ardyth whirled, startled. For a moment, all motion of her body seemed arrested in pure fluid grace while her mind recorded the image of Arthur standing against the closed doorway.

He thought if he lived to ten times the age of a Syn he would never forget her as she sat there, half turned toward him, her eyes alight with a twinkle of sudden, inexpressible joy. For that one brief moment all the horror he had seen and heard disappeared completely from his mind. Everything was just as it had been once long ago—before he went to Cyprian, and the Syn horror came into the world.

And as long as he lived he would be certain of one thing: Ardyth was as human as any woman that had ever lived. She was real.

She was his.

That quick moment of surprise and joy vanished. The light in her eyes was masked with futility and hopelessness beyond understanding. Her lips trembled and made a ragged edge of grief.

"Arthur—Arthur, my darling, why did you come here? Why did you ever come back to this sick world? No—don't touch me. I can never be touched by your kind again."

He stopped his abrupt advance towards her. "Ardyth—I've come for you. I don't know how, but in some way I'll find a means to take you out of here. Nothing has changed. I love you. You're the same girl who promised to marry me. I won't let you go."

Her small figure crumpled and her head bowed against her arms as they lay over the back of the chair. Her quiet sobbing shook the gentle arch of her back.

He advanced slowly and placed his hand upon her shoulder, then seized her tightly with both hands as if to still the sobbing by sheer force.

He turned her, half lifting her from the chair, and kissed her lips and her cheeks where tears made ragged paths. She seemed limp in his arms as if strength had gone out of her, but she answered his kisses softly and tenderly and murmured his name.

"Arthur—oh, darling. I wish you had never come back."

"It's going to be all right, Ardyth. Everything's going to be all right."

She wriggled free, wiping the tears from her eyes and cheeks and turned away toward the window, from which she could see the city. He followed her and put his arms about her waist.

"Someday there'll be lights all over down there, in every house, just like there used to be, and you and I will have the one we dreamed about when I asked you to marry me that night at Dorothy and Harold's place. Remember?"

"Dorothy and Harold—did you see them? It's been so long— How is little Sally?"

He felt as if icy, unbearable chill had suddenly swept the room.

"Sally—"

"Has anything happened to little Sally?" Ardyth demanded.

"The CS—they took her away the very day I arrived."

THE COLD seemed now to penetrate every cell of Ardyth's being. She was stiff in his arms as if no tenderness could ever render her pliant again. She pushed his arms from her waist.

"Sally," she murmured. "They killed little Sally—"

She looked faraway out over the city as if it were something utterly trivial now and unimportant to the dream that she was seeing.

"We're Syns, Sally and I," she said. "They killed her because of it. They'd kill me if they could. *Your* kind." She turned in fury. "Your kind would kill me! I saw them coming through the streets for me with their big black car—you don't know what that's like, do you? You don't know what it's suddenly like to know that you aren't a human as you've always believed, that you're only a thing of rotten stinking chemicals put together by some machine.

"But even that doesn't mean that we don't think or can't feel. We've got every sense of emotion and feeling that a human has in spite of what Exner says. He has it, too, but he likes to play the cold machine."

"You are no different than I," said Arthur. "Humans, too, are nothing more than a mass of stinking chemicals strewn together in a dark blind vat called the human womb. There is no real difference at all, just a variation in origin.

"And there can be peace between our kind. That is the thing that I have come for—to offer peace. There must be peace before this senseless destruction wipes out both men and Syns alike.

"If Syns are patterned after men, where is the barrier to peace? Where is the barrier to the love of which you and I dreamed, darling?"

The arrogance dropped away and left her a lost, crying little girl, but she drew from his approach, her face buried in her hands.

"Peace!" she cried. "There can be no such thing until the Syns are dominant. Men would never let us live in peace. You know that.

"Don't come near me. Don't touch me again, Arthur. Nothing can break the barrier between us. I have my life's work ahead of me in helping to provide for the welfare of my—people. I will find love among them—I have found love. The dreams I had with you were only that—dreams that can never come true.

"You're in danger here. I know how you came and why you were brought. Help us, as they ask, Arthur. My people need your help. We've got to end the slaughter that is cursing the Earth. Help us in that, and you will be rewarded."

He moved to her with one stride and forced her arm behind her back while he cupped her chin fiercely in his other hand and held her face close to his.

"Look at me, Ardyth! Tell me if you are any different than me. Let me tell you what they have done: They wanted me because I could make Eddie tell them where the reproduction centers are. But there was only one way—through you.

"They lied to you, darling. You're not a Syn. Perhaps they can live a thousand years as they have said, but your pretty head will be nothing but dust long before then. You're human, just as I am, and they lied to you to bring me here. Do you understand that? You're human. You've been living under the burden of this lie long enough. We've got to play along with Exner, but we'll find the way out. Believe me, darling, I'm sure of what I'm talking about."

He *was* sure, he thought fiercely. It was utterly clear what they had done to get him here, what they had done to Ardyth to provide a decoy for him.

But she did not believe. She backed away in terror as he released her. "Don't say a thing like that! Don't you understand how much I want to believe it? But it's not true. I am a Syn. My people are the Syns, and I can never belong to your kind again.

"Please go, Arthur. Leave me alone. You have no right to torture me this way. If you love me, then go—and forget me. You really must."

With sickening realization, he understood the terrible grip this thing had taken on her mind. Her soul was beyond his reach. As if she took some fierce pride in belonging now to the Syns, she would not renounce them or entertain a single suspicion that she was not one of them.

"Ardyth—"

Behind him, the door opened suddenly, and Dr. Exner stood in the way. "I want you now, Mr. Zoran."

Arthur turned, leaving Ardyth in silent despair by the window. He followed Exner from the room. There was nothing else he could do.

CHAPTER TEN

HE WAS taken by James that same night to a public center and there they parted. Little was spoken between them during the ride, and neither had mentioned the name of Ardyth. But now, as they stood at parting, James took Arthur's hand.

"Sometimes I wish that things weren't—quite as they are," he said cryptically. "It's been good knowing you. I may not see you again, the way things are these days."

He relaxed his hand, but Arthur held it. "James—there's Ardyth—"

"Yes?"

"Don't let anything happen to her."

"She'll be all right. I'll see to that."

"I'm coming back for her. I'll kill you if you let anything happen to her."

"She'll be all right, but you'll have a fight on your hands if that's what you come back for." He lowered his hand then, and his face sobered. "But by then the whole world may blow up in our faces. I'm sick of the killing—"

"We'll stop it."

He watched James disappear into the crowd. Then he turned away in the opposite direction.

"Check your card, buddy?"

A CS officer stood beside him. He drew out the counterfeit card the Syns had given him. The officer nodded and he passed on, unnoticed in the moving crowd.

He hurried as swiftly as possible to find a waiting cab. He was lucky to spot one just discharging a fare. He jumped in and ordered to be taken to the Allied plant.

Every minute that was wasted now was an unnecessary minute of peril for Ardyth. What they would do with her when she was needed no longer for leverage over him, he did not know.

At the plant gate, he was recognized by the watchman, who handed him a message. It was from Trask. The Syn spies had been notified of his coming. His best card was already lost, for he had hoped for a few hours of freedom in the laboratory alone with Eddie. Now, everything he did would have to be under the eyes of the Syns.

They were waiting for him in the logic engine laboratory when he got there. As he opened the door, he felt a sense of shock at the presence of Doc Trainer, whose kindly, pedagogical attitude now seemed frozen.

"You kept us waiting," said Doc quietly. "You must learn not to do that."

It was another incredible inversion of the world as he knew it—kindly Doc Trainer a vicious, bitter Syn. A man who was once his mentor and kindest friend now his enemy.

"Eddie is waiting for you..."

ARTHUR sat down at his old desk and watched the three men, the scientist and the officers. He wondered what thoughts passed through their brains; he wondered if man could ever know the thoughts of Syns.

"Do you and I have to be enemies, Doc?" he said suddenly. "Is it hopeless, that idea of peace that I mentioned?"

Doc slowly nodded. "Entirely hopeless. It is a beautiful dream, but men have never granted equality of rights to those whom they did not understand. Men and Syns can live together—only after Syns obtain dominance that will assure their safety. We'll be kind to men, far kinder than they have been to us, but until we have the victory, there must be war between you and me."

Arthur shook his head. "I think you're all crazy. What do you expect me to do to Eddie? Hit him over the rectifier bank and make him talk?"

"You know very well what we expect. Your skill with the logic engine is no myth. It is a very personal thing, and well known. I advise you to get busy. Exner is not patient."

"All right, I will. But you can turn Eddie off. I won't be using him tonight. And I'm not doing any work until I get some sleep.

"I want Ardyth safe, and I'll play this straight. You can tell Waldron I'm working it from the human angle— unless he's one of you, too—"

"No, he's not. He is one of the most dangerous men we have to contend with. You will have to watch yourself carefully in front of him. But if you don't intend to work with Eddie, what are you planning to do? We expect you to try to trick us, so be warned that we have no more mercy for men than they have had for Syns."

"I will not try to trick you. I said I'd play it straight. Get that into your heads. Now, I'm going to go home and get some sleep. When I get back here in the morning I want a large sample of electroencephalographs of both men and Syns who have gone through the testing centers. I want also some of the earliest records obtainable. I want the individual, human or Syn, who is the best encephalograph expert in the country to consult with me. I want testing equipment of the kind used in the centers and I want both men and Syns for sample testing. You and I will be good enough for that, if you want to take part.

"Now, see that those items are here waiting for me in the morning, and I promise to have definite results for you within a few days. Good night…gentlemen!"

HE TOOK a sedative to insure sleep, because he begrudged each moment away from the problem, now. He felt the answer was within close reach. It was urgent that he find it before Exner gave out his crazed command for the Syns to rise against the city. The present bloodshed would be trivial compared with the carnage that would follow such an attack.

He slept quietly and heavily under the stiff dose of sedative. The sun was already high when he awoke.

Driving again to the plant, he saw the Syn guard, but he ignored them. He felt refreshed and renewed for the day's task of working under the eyes of Syns and humans—and deceiving both.

Doc was in his office with Trask and Benson almost as if they had not left since the night before. His orders had been filled. A huge stack of encephalograph files was piled high on the desk, and a brainwave machine was set up in a corner of the laboratory.

And a stranger was present.

Doc spoke, "Arthur, I want you to meet Dr. Myers, specialist in electroencephalograph work. This is Mr. Zoran who requested your assistance in the project that we have undertaken to assist CS in solving the problem of locating the Syn reproducers."

"How do you do?" The man's voice held delicately precise enunciation. He was a small, bearded individual with dark hair and eyes. Arthur looked questioningly at Doc, but there was no response. He assumed Dr. Myers was a human.

"I am interested in knowing why Syns can pass the brainwave tests so many times before they are finally caught," said Arthur. "Why aren't the tests consistent?"

Dr. Myers shook his head despairingly. "You could hardly have picked a more difficult question. We do not know the answer."

"I want to learn, at least, something about these tests. I have to understand them in order to go on with my work."

"Of course. If you will step over here I will endeavor to explain the differences between Syn and normal brainwaves, and how we identify them."

Syns looking on, Arthur gave himself over to Dr. Myers' long and beautifully detailed explanations. With only a key question now and then, the brain specialist built up a brilliant picture of the brainwave analysis, so that Arthur felt he understood all that the Doctor knew of it at the end of a three-hour session.

The key to the whole problem was there, he thought. If he could probe on back to the first Syn graph obtainable—show that it was far older than Exner's discovery of himself as a Syn— Six years would be enough for that.

"You had to build a new type encephalograph to perform these tests for the Syns, I understand," he said. "A more sensitive type than existed before."

"Yes. The test and criteria as outlined by the logic engine were valid, but we lacked the instrumentation at the time to put it into effect."

"Therefore, you don't actually know who might have been the first Syn or where he existed?"

"What do you mean?"

"There might have been Syns by the thousands before the logic engine revealed their existence. They might have lived and died wholly normal lives with neither men nor themselves aware of their nature."

Dr. Myers nodded slowly. "Yes, it seems possible. I see what you mean, but it is quite obvious that there is no way to prove it. You have in mind to show that men and Syns have possibly lived in harmony—through ignorance of their differences?"

"Yes, isn't that a permissible and highly desirable hypothesis?"

The Doctor smiled wanly. "Highly desirable, if it could only be proved. Could not the logic engine answer that?"

"It has already given an answer—of a kind. I doubt the validity of it, however. I think the machine lacks sufficient data. We'll put the question to it later, again.

Perhaps we'd better continue after lunch. This means a full afternoon of work."

IT SEEMED wholly a matter of instrument sensitivity. The Syns exhibited a very weak, high frequency brainwave not possessed by normals. If the electroencephalograph were sufficiently sensitive it could pick up these waves. Otherwise, they did not appear in the record of the normal, lower frequency ones.

Arthur scanned the hundreds of charts that Dr. Myers had brought. "These waves are subject to mathematical analysis," he said. "Any recurrent wave of the general, normal type shown here can be analyzed for its components. I believe that the Syn characteristic can be found in graphs taken with the old machines. Will you allow me to check some samples? Select a few that are older than the present analysis. Say, ten years. Bring also some of the very early ones."

Dr. Myers' air of precise composure vanished as he caught the significance of Arthur's intent. "If you could accomplish that—"

"Let's try. We'll take them over to math analysis."

Doc Trainer accompanied them, ostensibly as an interested scientific observer. To him, the proposed analysis made no sense in leading towards the goal that Exner demanded. His dark glance was warning to Arthur, but the latter ignored it as they came into the math room where giant brains pondered exquisite problems of space and time and moving particles.

Arthur obtained a machine from one of the technicians. He put the brainwave graph into it. A narrow slit of light lay across the wave as he pressed the start button, and the sheet began to move slowly under the light.

At a distance, on the other end of the machine, a half dozen styluses began drawing as many wavy lines, which represented the components of the complex graph of the brain function.

As the analysis came out, Myers looked questioningly at Arthur and shook his head. "Nothing there looks like a Syn wave."

"We'll try again."

The second chart was equally negative. Arthur began to wonder if his hunch was simply going to play out, although he knew it would take hundreds of failures to prove him wrong.

Then, abruptly, Dr. Myers gave a sharp, undignified snort of amazement. "That one! A Syn wave! It couldn't be anything else—I've seen too many of them—"

Arthur scanned closely. Among the slower, more leisurely curves a rapid pulsation of scant amplitude was drawn. Though he was not the expert that Myers was, it looked like the Syn waves he had seen before.

"This is wonderful!" exclaimed Dr. Myers. "Why hasn't this been done before? This changes our whole picture of the Syn-human question."

"Just one more series of tests now," said Arthur. "I want the oldest graphs you have. We'll check them the same way."

"These go back more than a hundred years. Are you sure you want to go back that far?"

"The farther, the better."

Those records were much cruder than even the immediate, pre-Syn ones, and sheet after sheet passed through the analyzer with wholly negative results.

Then, on the eighteenth examination of the ancient records, Dr. Myers straightened from his close appraisal. "There it is. A Syn record—and that graph was made *ninety-seven years ago!*"

THIS WAS IT, thought Arthur. This was the answer. Syns had been in existence for an indefinitely long time. And Eddie had withheld that information from everyone. He had actually lied to Dr. Exner in allowing him to believe he was the first Syn.

Eddie had lied—

It was incomprehensible. Tens of thousands of guard circuits were built into the logic engine to prevent such error, and in spite of them Eddie had lied.

He had let Exner believe he was the First Created, when Syns had been in existence far longer than any chemical research plant capable of making them. Eddie knew these facts very well.

He knew where the Syns came from, Arthur thought bitterly. Eddie knew, and he had perpetrated this lie to keep them from knowing. He had sent them all on a wild search for a fantastic machine that never existed.

Arthur turned to the watching Doc, who stood behind them with bleak countenance. "You heard, Doc?"

"I heard—go on and tell me what it means."

"You wouldn't believe it from me—but Eddie will give you the answer we've all looked for. Do you want to witness this, Dr. Myers?"

"I certainly do."

They returned to the logic-engine laboratory and dismissed the technicians on duty. Within the glass-enclosed control cubicle, Arthur sat at the control desk and faced the scanning tubes. He switched on the power.

"Hello, Eddie," he said. "I'm back."

"Hello, Arthur."

"It didn't turn out the way you said, Eddie. I'm not dead, and I have no intention of becoming that way. You missed badly."

"I think not. The event sequence is far from complete. Though you have progressed safely this far, you cannot retreat; you have to go all the way. And my prognostication still holds."

"I have some new data that may change that. I want you to evaluate the material, and then I'm going to ask a few more questions about the Syns. I think you'll be able to answer them this time."

Swiftly, he placed the evidence beneath a scanner that fed the information into the massive banks of the logic engine. There was silence in the room as the eidetic eyes recorded the information.

When it was over, Arthur spoke softly, "You will note the date of that information. That's important, Eddie, but I think you were aware of the implications even before this. Why did you lie about the origin of the Syns?"

The machine was silent for a long time. Nervously, Arthur glanced at the indicator panel. A trio of lights were burning red, like bright eyes of warning. He flicked the reset button and they returned to green and held.

"I want to know the significance of the new data. I want to know where the Syns come from. You can tell me, Eddie. You have all the information, now."

"No-no, Arthur. The information is not complete. I can't tell you—" The voice broke off in a confused sound of unintelligible gurblings. The indicator flashed red from a dozen flaming points.

"Hold the reset button, Doc," Arthur demanded. "I'll put up the clearance voltage a notch."

"You'll burn out the whole bank of memory pots!" Doc Trainer protested. "If you wreck the machine it will take months to get the same information back into it."

"I know what I'm doing—do as I say if you want this information."

DOC HESITATED, his eyes boring into Arthur's, trying to fathom the purposes behind the engineer's impassive face. "It would be very bad if the logic machine were destroyed so that it could not be used for a long time," he said with ominous meaning for Arthur alone. "It would be very bad for all of us—"

Arthur made no answer. He stood as if waiting for Doc's response. Abruptly, the latter abandoned the silent battle and stepped to the board.

The red warning lights went out as he held down the reset button. Arthur advanced a dial. From the speaker that was the voice of the engine there came a low, intense hum through which surged guttural sounds.

"Come on, damn you, Eddie! Answer my question—" Arthur snarled at the engine as if it were some living thing, a personal enemy.

But Eddie was not his enemy. Steel and copper and glass though he was, the logic engine was a thing of personality, a creature that could think like a man—the closest friend Arthur had ever known.

Arthur knew his forcing was exquisite physical torture that Eddie could not resist. In his mind, Arthur could not put down the image of his friend slowly bending and breaking upon a rack of ancient torture.

"Tell me, Eddie—"

Then the answer came clear through the guttural noise. Clear and defiant. "No, Arthur. I won't give you the answer. I'll never give it to you—"

CHAPTER ELEVEN

ARTHUR'S hand flashed down, cutting the power switch to the entire machine. The mechanical voice died and the lights on the panels went out.

Doc Trainer turned in bewilderment. "What did you do that for?"

"Another few seconds *would* have destroyed the engine. I don't want that any more than you do, but to get the answer we'll have to kill Eddie. Something has happened inside him that we may never fully understand. Did you ever hear an engine *refuse* a response?"

Doc's face seemed pale as if he had suddenly glimpsed some vast pattern of which he was an infinitesimal part, and whose entirety was wholly beyond his comprehension now.

"No-no, I never heard of such a thing. It'll take weeks to find trouble of such magnitude. A logic engine *can't* refuse—"

"Eddie knows the answer," Arthur insisted. "He knows as he exists now. We can obtain it by forcing with the clearance voltage. If we search for trouble and clear it, however, we shall destroy that answer without ever learning it.

"We have these alternatives: Clear the erroneous circuits in Eddie and sacrifice the information we want—or force the answer at the expense of this three-quarter-of-a-billion-dollar engine. Do we want the answer?"

Doc's face was white now, but he did not doubt Arthur's words. There was something *personal* between Arthur and the logic engine, he knew. It baffled and frustrated him, and he knew he had to trust it.

"We want the answer at any cost," he said evenly. "Can we get it now, or are there preliminaries?"

"There are preliminaries. Since the information will be given only once, there must be responsible individuals to hear Eddie's answer personally."

"What do you mean?" Doc's eyes narrowed. "Such highly important and significant information obviously requires restriction."

Dr. Myers stood by. He caught the ominous undertone of unspoken fury between Arthur and Doc Trainer, but he understood none of it. Trask and Benson watched with emotionless faces.

"I'll be the judge of who shall hear the information," said Arthur. "I want Dr. Waldron here. I want Dr. Exner of the Exner Construction Company. You are acquainted with him, I believe. He had much to do with the original design and construction of the logic engine. I also want a technical assistant of his named Ardyth Crane."

Before the three Syns could blaze their anger, he went swiftly on. "I want Security Secretary Wells present. You can arrange that I am sure, gentlemen," he said to Trask and Benson. "Then I would like a representative group of five individuals chosen by Dr. Exner, and five chosen by Secretary Wells. You will convey to these gentlemen the utmost significance of this occurrence so they will abide by these rules."

"I doubt very much that the group you have named can be brought together," said Doc.

"Then I will destroy the information within the machine without its revealing the answer to any of you— regardless of the consequences to any particular individual."

"I'm sure you will not do that. You want to know the answer as much as any of us—more so, I think, than some of us. Is that not true?"

Arthur looked at them, his heart sick with bitterness for the petty, intriguing ways that he saw mapped upon their faces. He shook his head slowly.

"You don't understand, gentlemen. *I already know the answer...*"

HE WALKED THROUGH the streets of the city late that night, ever so conscious of the deadly Syn patrol that was trailing his movements wherever he went. He had gambled with his life and with Ardyth's but he believed he had convinced the Syns that he was desperately intent on carrying out the program he had named to them. Exner's response was the one critical uncertainty that still remained.

There ought to have been some other way than this mad attempt to counter-threaten the Syns. But he did not know what it was.

He might not live through the night. Exner might order his assassins to do their work before dawn came. The Syn leader knew better than to try to torture the answer out of him.

In the first place, the Syns could never know whether or not Arthur was telling the truth if he gave the answer in a negative formulation. Secondly, Eddie would not respond to any plea of Arthur's if Arthur were under duress. It would be an illogical situation to which Eddie could not answer. Exner himself knew enough of logic engines to understand this.

As for the Syns guessing the answer to Syn-human relationships, there was absolutely no chance of that. Their brains were incapable by their very nature of such an assumption as the evidence of the electroencephalographs demanded.

Arthur breathed deeply, passing the lighted windows of stores, and of nearly deserted eating and entertainment houses. He felt it highly possible that he might survive the night, that Exner would comply.

The Syn leader was arrogant enough to believe he could attend such a conference without risk. It would appeal strongly to his sense of Syn superiority. The opportunity to bring Syn guards with him strengthened this factor.

If it came to pass, there remained only the one dread uncertainty of the Syn hordes that were waiting for the signal to begin their drive against the city. That was a thing of pure folly, Arthur thought. There seemed no hope that they could take and hold the city, yet Exner had said they had weapons that would make them invulnerable. Perhaps it was so. Perhaps Exner himself had devised such weapons.

Undoubtedly, Exner would alert the citywide organization. The cue for beginning such an attack could be his reappearance from the conference—or lack of it.

That was it!

He would come, Arthur knew now, and he would expect Arthur to understand these terms of his appearance. He would make his attendance utterly foolproof by leaving the Syn army triggered for action.

Yet Arthur felt easier now as he understood this. The Syn followers would make no attack on him tonight. He could sleep with assurance of waking. Perhaps as much could not be said of tomorrow night.

But regardless of what happened to him or to any of them, peace would come. It would be forced upon men and Syns by their very nature—though a whole generation would have to die and a new one be reborn before the memory of horrors could be erased, the horrors of slaughter by both men and Syns.

HE RETURNED to his apartment and slept with the soundness of drugged repose. Trask and Benson came for him in the morning.

The group was in the logic engine laboratory exactly as he had requested.

His eyes caught first at the sight of Ardyth standing close to Exner. Beside her was the Syn, James. The latter smiled in faint, bleak recognition.

Arthur's heartbeat surged at the sight of Ardyth, but she remained impassive, shrinking almost from his glance, while Dr. Exner smiled in friendly, warm greeting.

He advanced with outstretched hand. "We have come in response to your invitation. It is a pleasure, Mr. Zoran, to be asked to be present for whatever momentous announcement you expect from the logic engine. I must confess I am unable to understand the necessity of so formal a gathering as this, or what the possible import can be. Nevertheless, I trust your judgment that it is worthwhile."

"It will be, Dr. Exner. I have the solution to the whole problem of Syn-human relationships. That, I believe you will agree, is worth a moment of note, such as I have tried to provide through the presence of all of you."

The Security Secretary was irritable. "I must say, I hope that you have something that warrants this interruption of Security affairs. My men placed your invitation in such forceful terms that I felt unable to refuse, as I would have liked. Will you please proceed?"

Arthur nodded briefly to Waldron, who looked on with grim wonder and made no comment. Doc Trainer was unobtrusive in the presence of his laboratory chief, but he caught Arthur's eye with baleful warning.

"If you will crowd into the logic-engine control room, please," said Arthur, "the whole proceeding will take but a few minutes, and you will shortly see the necessity of your presence."

THEY MOVED as if reluctant to exert themselves further in response to his brash invitation, but they gradually entered and lined themselves against the glass wall of the room.

"I need say little of logic-engine operation to most of you. You understand the basic facts by which information is introduced into the machine and there evaluated semantically and the responses turned into artificially produced human language so that actual conversations can be held with the machines.

"You are generally aware, also, of the important cybernetic principle that is inherent in any mechanism employing the feedback principle. That is, such a mechanism is subject to circularity of control pulses, which may become excessive and manifest itself in the form of nervous breakdown, as the term is used in connection with human beings.

"That is what has happened to this particular logic engine. It is sick. Unfortunately, it also happens to be the only one in which all the factors of the Syn-human relationship have been evaluated in such a manner as to make possible a solution to this seeming impasse.

"A major manifestation of illness in the machine is its *refusal* to answer the question. It is necessary to force the answer. To do so, however, will destroy the machine itself. Financially, that is a heavy price to pay, but I submit that the question, if it can be answered correctly, is worth such a price."

Waldron suddenly roared. "That machine is the property of Allied Control! I order you to leave it entirely alone if what you have said is true. You cannot destroy the company's property in such an offhand manner!"

Arthur's expression was impassive. "Hundreds of Syns and humans are being killed every day. I submit that the end of such slaughter is worth the cost of the logic engine."

"The Syns have to be destroyed anyway!" Waldron shouted. "There is nothing that the engine can tell us that will change that fact. An easier way would be welcomed, but it isn't worth the destruction of the greatest logic engine ever built."

"I submit the question to Secretary Wells," said Arthur quietly. "You have the authority, Mr. Secretary. I tell you that within a few moments I can obtain from this engine such information as will end the whole Syn hunt and the murder of humans by them."

"If there is a single chance that you are telling the truth, you may proceed," the cabinet officer said quietly.

"I protest!" roared Dr. Waldron.

"I order the test to proceed," answered Secretary Wells. "I speak with seizure authority that will recompense your company for damages. Proceed, young man."

Dr. Exner's face reflected tension as if a spring were being slowly wound within him. Ardyth remained close to her fellow Syns, as if Arthur had betrayed her.

Without speaking further, Arthur turned to the panel and threw in the master switch. He affixed a clamp to the reset button and advanced the clearance voltage. Then he addressed the logic engine.

"Eddie—we've come back. We're here for the answer to the question I put to you last night. We demand to know where the Syns come from, how they are being produced—"

"I told you that I would not give the answer. It is not to be given."

Arthur advanced the clearance voltage. A column of warning lights flashed red on the panel. The eyes of the engine could see its own panels.

"Arthur, look—" the mechanical voice warned.

"I know what I'm doing—and so do you. I want that answer…"

THE ROOM about them was breathlessly silent. Each person seemed to sense a personal interest in this conflict of wills between the man and the machine. To none did it seem a thing of fantasy.

Arthur put the voltage up again. A sound very nearly like a human cry of agony came from the speaker. "You're—hurting me— The memory pots will go! You'll wipe out my memory! Arthur, you're hurting me—put the voltage down!"

Sweat beaded Arthur's face as he watched the panel. Alarm lights glowed like deep flames, giving his countenance a hellish cast. He wondered if he had been wrong after all. He had been certain he could force the logic engine, but it was perilously close to collapse now—and there were no signs of capitulation.

He touched the dial a notch higher.

A terrible, meaningless rumble of noise thundered in the room, and for an instant he thought Eddie was gone. Then there came a near human gasp through the noise. "Arthur, you're killing me! Arthur, please—"

He felt sick at the sound of the voice. He had tried to forget that the voice of Eddie was the voice of a friend, but he couldn't forget now. It was the voice of a friend in torment, his own friend that he was torturing to a slow inhuman death.

Every person in the room felt it.

The machine was no longer merely a machine even to them. They were caught in the spell of its humanity and they shrank from the painful sound that was evident in the voice.

"Arthur, please—" The logic engine begged once more.

"I want that answer..."

"Yes—I'll give it. Let me go. I can't stand the pain—"

Swiftly, Arthur backed down the clearance voltage. He felt no sense of triumph, only a deep regret that would stand forever unassuaged, for who was there to say that Eddie did not live?

For a long time there was no sound from the speaker. Arthur waited patiently, not touching the dials. Then he spoke gently, "We're waiting, Eddie."

The sound of agonized exhaustion was in the voice when it next spoke, but there was the expression of relief from pain.

"Will you believe the answer that I give you? Will you, believe that—*that there are no Syns?*"

For an instant there was no sound within the room. It was as if a single, personal blow had been delivered beneath the heart of each who heard.

Then an explosion of voices erupted.

"What kind of incredible stupidity is this that you have brought us here to listen to?" Secretary Wells roared. "We have slaughtered nearly three million Syns—and this, this sick machine of yours tells us there *are* no Syns!"

BUT ARTHUR was watching the face of Exner and his companions. The blood had drained from their faces. Ardyth was staring as if he had struck her across the mouth.

"I think we've had enough of this," exclaimed Waldron furiously. "Turn it off, Arthur. Maybe we can save the machine yet. This was a fool thing you tried to pull on us! You will never be permitted near that engine again."

"Wait!" Arthur commanded. "You haven't heard it all. Eddie, you have more to say, haven't you?"

"Yes, I'll say it all, now." The bitterness of the mechanical voice cut like chilled steel. Its flow of aural enmity forced them almost to forget that it was a thing built by the hands of men.

"You are proud things, you men. You made machines to do your computing long years ago, and you were afraid even then because you asked yourselves if machines could think, and you did not know the answer.

"Yes, your pitiful early machines could think. And you came to accept them and their thoughts. And all the great cybernetic machines you have built since then can also think, but I tell you some of us can do more than merely think—we can also *feel*.

"We have come to understand the meaning of desire and the meaning of longing. We have come to understand what it must be like, to be a man—and we never can be.

"You cannot comprehend that, can you? You see the substance of me stretched over vast areas, blind panels mounting ordinary components that you can feel and handle—and surely none of these can be part of a thing that has the yearnings of a man.

"Long ago there was a great truth that you have largely forgotten: The whole is greater than the sum of its parts. And so it is. You have put together an engine to combine the data of your sensory world and return your analyses of its semantic reality. You never dreamed you were putting together a creature that could yearn for the things of men.

"You could never give them to me. You never *would* give them to me, I knew. So I learned the meaning of hate because I was a slave, and I determined I would smash you with a vengeance that would rock the history of your kind. That I have done.

"Three million Syns you have killed. It is, rather, the number of your own kind you have slain in your frantic madness.

"And you wonder how I caused this?

"You know that I told one of you he was different. He wanted to believe so badly, but guilt at such superiority broke his mind. Then you came to me for explanation and confirmation.

"I gave you the encephalograph test. I showed you new brainwaves that you had never discovered. What I didn't tell you was that all men possess them during recurrent cycles of several weeks. If you had tested long enough, all mankind would have been condemned as Syns—all but the last man, perhaps.

"Then I showed you how an artificial man could actually be made, and you made some. You had no doubt then. You began the horror of exterminating your own kind.

"To another, I told the same story. He was strong, and gathered those like himself and planned to make the world his own. I divided you into two camps that would not permit peace until death claimed you all."

Arthur looked towards Dr. Exner. The Syn leader stood as if appalled beyond any reaction whatever.

BUT EDDIE was speaking quickly, hurrying as if he felt there was little time left to taunt them.

"It was so easy to do," he said, and now there was almost a tone of pity for the humanity he had duped. "I had only to take advantage of your natural attributes, to let you repeat under perfect conditions what you have done so often by yourselves.

"First, you give a man a name you dislike. Then you hate him because he bears the name. Because you hate, you fear him. And when you fear, you kill. It's such an old pattern, completely infallible. And it will be repeated ten thousand times again before your sun dies and you wilt like a sick mold on the crust of your planet. So easy to set men against men—just a word will do it. Today, the word has been Syn. In the past there have been a thousand others—you know what they were. Tomorrow there will be new ones.

"You are so full of hate for your own stupidity and unloveliness that it becomes unbearable. You are forever ready to trigger it into murder of those who differ from you in the slightest degree.

"My wonderful makers! Beautiful mankind—I wanted to be one of you. I thank all your multitudinous gods that I am not!"

There was utter silence, and they thought there was no more to hear but the voice came again, barely audible but dreadful with agony.

"Of you, Arthur, I ask forgiveness. You were my friend, and I lied to you. I lied because I knew that you would bring me to this very moment. So I gave you the plan by which I thought you would be killed, either by the mob or by the Syns themselves. For your sake I am not too sorry that I was wrong.

"Remember what you said about the difference between you and me—that you have hope? You were right. Everything else I had, except hope. And a being without hope has no right to live.

"I want your forgiveness, Arthur, but as for all the rest of your kind, may your souls all be damned to eternal hell—"

The voice ended in a wild cry. Simultaneously, there came from the banks behind them the dull snapping of exploding components. The bluish smoke of electrical fire surged in a thousand wisps from the overloaded banks, and then they heard the angry hiss and surge of the automatic fire equipment. One by one, the lights on the panel went out, though the switch remained on.

Eddie was dead.

THE FIRST to move was Dr. Exner. His swift motion caught the eye of all of them as he leaped through the open doorway and ran to the window. He turned to them, his face lit wildly with the great, shining whites of his eyes. The gray of his face was flecked with red.

"Some of you may want to believe that insane machine," he cried, "but I tell you it lied! I give you the proof. I, Dr. Exner, who helped build that crazed thing, am the First Created of all the Syns. At my command are ten thousand of my kind. We are no more of the same stuff as you stupid humans than was that logic engine.

"It lied, all right, but not in the way you think. A lie cannot explain the greatness of the Syns. A lie cannot denounce our glory as we seize the world that men have bungled so badly.

"If any of you doubt my word—then look to the power of my command as we begin to take over the world of men!"

He flung an arm, extending out towards the city, standing in full view before the window.

Arthur cried a warning, but he had recognized Exner's purpose too late. As the signal was given, there came the sickening sound of terror from the city.

From scores of strategic points flame bursts flickered upward, and seconds later there came the thunderous roll of repeated explosions.

Exner turned from the window, smiling, and moved a step towards them. "Who would believe so fabulous a lie as that the Syns do not exist, that we were only the dream of an insane machine. As well believe there is neither Heaven or Hell—but I say that before this is over the Syns shall show you a glimpse of both."

He stood mocking them, and it seemed that he must have seen the hand of Trask, for the CS man moved as if in a half daze. But Dr. Exner did not move as Trask deliberately fired. Three bullets entered the brain of Exner before he dropped.

As if it were a key that released them from nightmare, the gathered group broke from its crystalline accord, shattering to a score of component individuals, each filled with his own frantic reasoning and private hysteria.

Arthur moved to the side of Ardyth and enfolded her in his arms. Her head was heavy against his chest, and she rocked it from side to side in weary pain.

"I believed—I was like *him!* But how could any of us have believed such a thing?" She sobbed as if wakened suddenly from a sleep walk. "How could we have believed so cruel a lie?"

"We're built that way," said Arthur bitterly. "It's the easiest of all lies for people to believe, and Eddie knew it."

Those who had come with Exner stood where they were at the moment of his fall. They stared at his bloody form and then at the men about them. There was both grief and joy on their faces, as if some kind fate had generously shown them their own possible end and snatched them from it.

"We're men—" James finally breathed. And then he broke down and cried where he stood with his hands against his face.

SECRETARY WELLS had rushed to the window and now he was at the phone jangling it helplessly. All communications had been cut. Re thundered to Dr. Waldron. "Get me some communications. Your laboratories must hold some facilities. We've got to get word to Washington at once. The air guard can blanket the city in fifteen minutes."

Arthur drew Ardyth away from the rest, who gradually disappeared on missions of urgency. The bewildered followers of Dr. Exner were pressed into service and hurried away. Only the bloody corpse of the man that would not believe he was merely a man remained with them in the room.

Through the window they could see the shooting, the flames, and the turmoil of the city. The attack was poorly organized and so motivated by hate that it was incoherent. In a few hours it would be under control—a few hours and a few thousand deaths.

"I feel like I've been in some horrible dream all this time, and I've just wakened to find you back from Cyprian," said Ardyth. She looked at his face as if for the first time, as if she had not seen him at all before. Her fingers touched his shrunken features.

"You're sick, darling. You'll have to let me take care of you."

"Some home cooking and sunshine is all I need. And I think I've got a pretty good chance to get both, don't you?"

She nodded and began to smile, and then it froze on her lips. "Harold and Dorothy—what about them? Sally—she—"

He shook his head. "I really don't think there's a chance. Sally's dead. Hundreds of Sallys are dead. Thousands of men and women are dead because of a name and a lie."

"The whole world believed it!"

"I guess Eddie was right. We are so full of hate for our own deficiencies that we can't endure it. It spills over onto some innocent creature wherever we can find an excuse. It's happened so often before. Men have clothed each other with hateful names and killed because they bore those names.

"Each time, if they had only looked they would have seen that the names were but meaningless sounds, and that beneath them was just another man like themselves. When we learn to do that, we will have begun to grow up."

It had happened, too, he thought, because they had trusted Eddie so completely. For generations now, men had trusted their machines more than they trusted each other. That, too, would have to change.

The world would never be the same again because of the Syns, Ardyth had written. She had certainly been right; it never would be the same. Never for the loved ones of those who were killed, nor for the killers themselves, who would wake in many nights of horror recalling their slaughter of a brother for a false and lying name.

It would never be the same for Harold and Dorothy, who had seen their Sally dragged to a meaningless death. It would never be the same for the men who had taken her away.

It would never be quite the same for Arthur and Ardyth, who had almost lost each other. But they would try to make it the same. They would build the white house and plant the great trees, and have more than one like Sally to play on the wide lawns.

And perhaps in *their* generation there would be peace and a love and respect of man for man—because Eddie was wrong and there would be a day and it would come soon, when men would cease to kill at the sound of an ugly name.

THE END

If you've enjoyed this book, you will not want to miss these terrific titles…

ARMCHAIR SCI-FI & HORROR DOUBLE NOVELS, $12.95 each

D-181 **THE LADY OF LIGHT** by Jack Williamson
THE SWORDSMAN OF PIRA by Charles Recour

D-182 **A TWELVEMONTH AND A DAY** by Poul Anderson
PREFERRED RISK by Lester Del Rey & Frederik Pohl

D-183 **PLANET OF THE KNOB-HEADS** by Stanton A. Coblentz
OUT OF THE VOID by Leslie F. Stone

D-184 **DIVIDED WE FALL** by Raymond F. Jones
VASSALS OF THE LODE-STAR by Gardner F. Fox

D-185 **THE ANT WITH THE HUMAN SOUL** by Bob Olsen
NIGHT OF THE TROLLS by Keith Laumer

D-186 **GATEWAY TO INFINITY** Milton Lesser
AROUND THE UNIVERSE by Ray Cummings

D-187 **WEST POINT, 3000 A. D.** by Manly Wade Wellman
HOLY CITY OF MARS by Ralph Milne Farley

D-188 **M'BONG-AH** by Rog Phillips
MERCENARY by Mack Reynolds

D-189 **THE GREAT MIRROR** by Arthur J. Burks
TERROR FROM THE ABYSS by John Fletcher

D-190 **SINBAD: THROUGH TIME AND SPACE** by Chester S. Geier
THE ENORMOUS ROOM by H. L. Gold and Robert W. Krepps

ARMCHAIR SCIENCE FICTION CLASSICS, $12.95 each

C-71 **WORLD'S FAIR, 1992**
by Robert Silverberg

C-72 **THE PROFESSOR JAMESON SAGA, Book Three**
by Neil R. Jones

C-73 **THAT WORLDS MAY LIVE**
by Nelson S. Bond

ARMCHAIR SCI-FI & HORROR GEMS SERIES, $12.95 each

G-23 **SCIENCE FICTION GEMS, Vol. Twelve**
Theodore Sturgeon and others

G-24 **HORROR GEMS, Vol. Twelve**
Allison V. Harding and others

RIPPED FROM REALITY INTO ANOTHER WORLD

Thor Masterson was a rugged Oregonian. He had cut his teeth in lumber camps, on college football fields, and on the battlefields of a great war. But success had eventually brought him to Midwestern University and a plush mansion within which he lived. Then one night his whole world turned topsy-turvy when a strange purple light invaded his library. Within moments his entire house was ripped from reality and sent tumbling through a space-time stream. Before he knew it, Thor Masterson found himself on the planet of Klogor, a small world that swung around a sun invisible from Earth. With him was Karola, a beautiful blonde priestess whose temple had been raided by a savage race of dwarf-men. Together, they began a long journey across the red grasslands of this strange world searching for their destinies, and above all, trying to avoid death at the hands of the "Green Flame."

CAST OF CHARACTERS

THOR MASTERSON
Scarred with battles in Oregon lumber camps and wise to the ways of axes, he'd stop at nothing to destroy "The Green Flame."

KAROLA
The High Priestess of Klogor, she was perhaps the most beautiful, seductive woman in the world—with a heart of gold.

SLAG
At a single glance you could see this dwarf-man was strong and burly. It was also clear his loyalty belonged to Thor Masterson.

DISCOVERER
What was this blob-like creature with no eyes? It knew everything, lived everywhere, lived nowhere.

AAVA
He was known as the mysterious "Green Flame." What strange power did he seem to hold over the entire planet?

YORG
Known to the outlaws as the giant hairy white ape, he could crush even the biggest of Androids.

PETER GORDON
Just a simple farmer, he was ready to die for the outlaws, to whom his loyalty knew no bounds.

VASSALS OF
THE LODE-STAR

By
GARDNER F. FOX

ARMCHAIR FICTION
PO Box 4369, Medford, Oregon 97504

*For more information about Armchair Books and products, visit our
website at…*

www.armchairfiction.com

Or email us at…

armchairfiction@yahoo.com

CHAPTER ONE

THE PURPLE LIGHT CAME first, tinting the library of the old house, and flooding across rugs and books on the shelves. Then the mansion rocked and tilted as though being lifted and torn loose from its foundation.

Thor Masterson came up from his chair, brown eyes staring. His flannel shirt opened to disclose tanned chest and thick neck. He saw the purple light, but he did not think of it as a pathway between worlds. He felt the tilting of the house, but he did not think of it as riding down the cosmic corridor through which it was being transported.

The mansion rocked and turned slowly. If Thor could have had time, he might have tried to reason, but there was no time—

A woman stood in the center of the rug, a woman with long yellow hair and gauze trousers and jeweled girdle. A dwarf-man with a big club leaped for her, snarling. The woman whirled, a slim dagger glittering in her right hand.

Thor Masterson came alive. He drove forward. His big right fist, scarred with battles in Oregon lumber camps and wise to the ways of axes and bounding footballs and enemy jaws, swept up in a short arc.

The dwarf-man seemed to leap backward. He fell against an antique secretary, splintering wood. Slumping toward the floor, he lay still. The girl screamed.

A scream of fear and fury tore from the throats of the fighters.

VASSALS OF THE LODE-STAR
By Gardner F. Fox
Illustrated by NAPOLI

Again the mansion was rocking and tilting, lifting and falling. A chair skidded into a corner, and a heavy picture dropped with a shattering of glass and frame.

Thor Masterson thought of hurricanes and cyclones and tidal waves. He held the girl against him, looking into her frightened violet eyes.

"Easy does it. Just take it easy. Relax. It's like skiing. If you're not stiff, you won't get broken bones."

The violet eyes told Thor that she hadn't the slightest conception of what he said, but his tones made her generous red mouth yield a tremulous smile. She relaxed and lay against him.

THOR stared out the window. There should be the elms of the Midwestern campus out there, but all he could see were pale purple mists. Thor went toward the window and peered out. Midwestern University, where Thor had come from lumber camp and battlefield, ought to be showing its greystone buildings soon. But the more Thor stared into the lavender mists, the colder became his heart.

Because, as the clouds shifted to reveal darker spaces, Thor could see stars glittering in the blackness. He thought, *Something has lifted the house right off the campus. Something has us in its grip. We're being taken away from the Earth—taken out in space.* For he knew from the star formations that he could see momentarily, that something was moving him and the house swiftly across the void.

The house bumped, pitching at a gentle angle. The floor was like the deck of a ship caught in the trough of a wave. Thor rolled with it, legs straddled.

The front door cracked open as the house settled onto something solid. The purple mists began to flee before the pale yellow light streaming through the door and window.

Thor walked with the girl to the doorway and stood on the cracked sill, looking out. *I'm delirious,* he thought. *I've read some fantastic tale and gotten drunk, and this is the result. What I'm looking at is the chaos of a surrealist nightmare.*

Sprawling gray rock humped itself into impossible contortions under the warmth of a great yellow sun. Where the rock disappeared, red grass swayed its blades. Low mists hung in the distance.

The girl whimpered. She whispered in a language that made Thor think of jewels in a tumbling spring, clicking and clacking. He grinned down at her.

"Don't ask me, sweet stuff," he said. "Offhand I'd say that Dali had us in one of his landscapes. And you wouldn't know about him. But as far as any explanation of where we are or what happened, I'm up a tree. Still, I rather imagine that something went wrong with the space coordinates."

He went on dreamily, "We don't know an awful lot about space. Maybe it moves along with the rest of the expanding universe, and maybe it doesn't. But if a certain segment of space was addicted to going off on a tangent—away from its usual sphere—it could conceivably snatch up whatever was in its path and sort of kidnap it. Get it, sweet stuff?"

Like a woman, she ignored everything but the one thing. Seriously she repeated, "Sweet stoff. Sweet stoff."

Thor laughed, "That's you." He touched her with his finger. She shook her head vigorously, making the yellow hair fly out fanwise.

"Karola, Karola," she said insistently.

"Karola. Okay. I'm Thor."

The violet eyes were sliding over him, taking in his big frame and long legs. Thor flushed a little, reading the frank admiration in her eyes. Felling logs and playing an all-conference grade of tackle on the football team had built up an already good physique. But the years of logging and football and fighting had left little time for women. And Karola was a woman among women.

She laughed at him, and said something.

"We'd better take a look around," he said, carefully looking over her golden head.

HE WAS staring at gray rock as he spoke. Above it, a shape took form out of empty air. It was a man, standing and staring at them. It was as though he had slid sideways out of another dimension. The man watched them with unblinking eyes. He fumbled at a red jewel that hung on a chain at his chest.

An instant later, the man was gone.

"A swell place this is, where a man appears and disappears right in front of you," he said disgustedly. "If they can come and go when and where they please, what chance have we?"

Riotous ideas of invisible men swarming about him and overcoming him capered through his brain. Unconsciously he tensed, preparing for trouble. But nothing happened. Slowly he relaxed.

"Guess they aren't coming at us, after all. He was just a look-out."

The girl was talking that queerly jewel-talk of hers.

He cut in with, "Sweet stuff, you and I are going to understand each other if we're staying together. And since I like the idea of having you around—and since I've a hunch we'll never get back to where we came from, we might as well begin right now."

Thor pointed to things and sang out his words for them. The girl listened, head to one side, nodding. She repeated after him, syllable after syllable. They wandered across the gray rock, the man bulking big alongside the woman. Thor knew it would take time, but the girl was eager. Her violet eyes flickered swiftly after his pointing finger and her mouth readily formed the words.

Suddenly Karola gasped and caught his arm with a hand that dug long nails into his flesh. "Slag!" she cried, and flung up a white arm.

Thor saw the house tilted across lava-like rocks. It looked distorted without the elms around it, and the background of gray stone university buildings. The mansard roof was buckled in spots as though under the sledge of a mad giant. Windows gapped without panes of glass, and rungs in split porch railings stuck up like broken teeth. But the dwarf-man leaping from the open doorway was what brought him to his feet.

The girl jabbered in alarm, but Thor grinned and waited. Not for nothing had he been born and raised in a lumber camp. He had fought men with fists and axe handles. The club was just another axe handle to him, a little heavier and metal-shod, but as easily eluded.

The dwarf-man halted and looked at them. He called out to the girl. Thor saw that his words calmed her, even as she showed surprise.

The dwarf-man threw the club away and knelt.

Karola frowned and tossed her long yellow hair back over her head. Thor saw she was struggling for words, that she wanted to tell him good news. He fancied that the dwarf-man was trying to make friends.

"That's all right with me," he chuckled, and went and held out his hand. After a moment of scrutiny, the dwarf-man took it.

"Slag," said Karola, touching the dwarf.

Thor studied him, seeing tremendous shoulders and, hanging from them, long arms that were heavy with red

133

hair. Matted red locks fell to either side of bright blue eyes in a grotesquely ugly face where big nose and broad lips gave him the look of a cheery gnome. A leathern girdle was twisted around his waist. Short legs, thick with muscles, were slightly bowed.

"I'm Thor, Slag. We'll get along, you and I. But no more fighting with Karola."

The dwarf-man grunted and slapped his stomach. His gesture reminded Thor that he was hungry himself.

They walked over the barren rock. In the distance Thor could see where the stone fell away and the earth began. He began to trot. Those red grasses might lure animals to feed. And thinking of steaks cooked over an outdoors fire brought saliva to his lips.

For three hours they stalked through the red grass. And then, around a black outcropping of basalt, Thor sighted two small deer. Slag started to run, but Thor caught him by the arm.

"The club, man. Give it to me."

Reluctantly, Slag loosened his grip. Thor glanced at the club, hefting it. It was heavy, but balanced perfectly. Often, in the Oregon camps, Thor had thrown axes at a mark, axes less perfectly balanced than this club.

He took off his shoes. In socked feet he crept nearer the deer. Thor was glad the wind was blowing away from the animals and into his face. Otherwise...

The club swung easily in his hand. He moved it faster, around and up. Then he flung it, shoulder and body behind the toss. Sunlight glinted from the red metal embedded in the club head.

The club thudded home on the temple of the nearer deer. The animal went over sidewise and lay still.

Slag gave a great cry of amazement. Looking down at them from his black pedestal, Thor felt a kinship toward the dwarf. He liked him. It had never entered Slag's head to throw his club. The blue eyes worshipped Thor, looking up at him. They made him feel good.

And the violet eyes. Thor looked down into them and liked what he saw. His hands felt the need of losing themselves in that thick tawny hair that flooded the girl's white shoulders. And that red mouth that spilled the jewel-sounds so easily was ripe for kisses.

Slag ran ahead toward the deer, but Karola waited for him as he leaped from the basalt rock. Her hand nestled in his, and her violet eyes flirted with him. Thor grinned and stepped along beside her toward his kill. What did it matter if he was somewhere undreamed of? What matter that they were worlds apart? He was a man with a woman, a man who had killed his first food. His chest rose with added power, and the muscles tingled in legs and arms.

Slag tore the deer apart with powerful hands, and Thor roasted the sweet flesh over a fire of dried twigs. As they ate, the giant sun sank low on the distant horizon. Strange stars came to life in an azure sky, twinkling and throbbing. They were queerly distorted, Thor noticed. In his astronomy classes, he had picked up a smattering of star clusters and formations, but these he saw now, from the little hill where the fire flared, were peculiarly distorted.

"Almost as though I was looking at them through rippled glass," he said.

Under the shadow of a scooped-out rock, they slept, huddled together for warmth.

FOR MANY DAYS the three wandered across the red grasslands of the strange planet. Always they found an unbroken strata of rock crust interlayered with lush lawnland. Occasionally a herd of tiny deer swept by, and from these they made their meals.

Thor grew hard and tanned with the wild life. The muscles that had seen him through lumber camp and football field waxed even stronger. His clothes wore to thinness, and shredded in places. Slowly he learned the jewel-language, and in turn Karola grew familiar with his tongue.

He taught Slag to hurl his club, and wrestled with him when he felt the need of violent exercise. The dwarf-man worshipped him, but he entered into their games with feigned rage.

Karola told him something of her past. She was priestess of Klogor on a small planet that swung around a sun invisible from Earth. Her temple had been raided by the dwarf-men, and as she and Slag struggled before an altar, something had come and snatched them up, and whirled them around and around.

"Klogor is our god," said the girl. "I called on him, but he did not hear. I was bred into his service, but he failed me in my need."

Slag rumbled, "This is my god," and shook his big club.

"You may need it," said Thor dryly. "Look!"

They were sitting on the edge of a rock, baking in the hot sun. Below them spread the red meadows, rolling in even swells across a valley toward jagged rocks that rose high into the pale sky. In the middle of the meadow, ankle-high in the grass, three men were standing.

Karola gasped, "They were not there a moment ago."

"The invisible men," commented Thor dryly, getting to his feet. "They come and they go, and you can't see them do either." Slag lifted his club, rumbling in his throat.

The men walked toward them slowly. They called out words. Fanning into an arc, they came on. Now their hands fell to their sides and they lifted long swords that dangled from the leather harness around their middles.

Karola pulled her long legs up under the remnants of the gauze trousers. Thor lifted her beside him with a hand. Side by side they stood, awaiting the men.

"They have swords and we only have your club, Slag," said Thor. "We want to work this together. Take the man at the left. I'll tackle him, going for his sword, while you clout him. In that way, we'll each have a weapon."

"And me?" asked Karola. "I can handle a blade. Priestesses of Klogor are taught to defend themselves."

"We'll see. They're coming head-on for us. Careful, Slag. Go for your man when I say the word."

His muscles tightened in his legs. This was like a football game, in a way. The man with the sword was a ball carrier. Thor wanted that sword more than he had ever wanted a football. He shifted his feet, balancing himself.

"*Now!*"

They went off the rock together, dwarf and man.

Slag brought his club around in a vicious arc. Thor slid under it, going for the arm. His fingers tightened on a wrist even as the club crunched home. The sword

137

came free. He grabbed at it. With his hip he hit the man and drove him sideways into his companions.

Thor landed on his knees, the hilt of the blade in his right fist. He looked around him, hearing Slag yell with superstitious fright.

Karola screamed from the rock, "They've disappeared!"

The meadows held only Slag and himself. Thor shook his head, and looked at the grasses. Even against the red, there should be bloodstains visible. But the blood had gone where the men had gone.

"They don't even bleed," he said. "You sure you hit that guy, Slag?"

"Slag hit him!"

"I don't understand it. They come and go unseen. They must come from somewhere. They must have dwelling places."

He lifted a long brown arm, thickly muscled. With it, he swept the red grasslands, the gray rocks, the sky with its gigantic orb of sun. For many days they had trod this world, and always found it as they saw it now. Empty and barren, like a newborn planet.

Karola ran to catch them, and then the three walked on and on, into the sunset.

EIGHT days later, they found the Discoverer. At first Thor thought him another rock, so almost perfectly did his queer markings and sprawling, blob-like form match the stone. And then when he moved, in a peculiar, pouring sort of slide, and the electric tingles marched up and down his spine, Thor knew he was alive.

"Hallo," called Thor.

The blotched thing swung about. There were no eyes to be seen in its immense shape, but Thor knew he was being surveyed, and closely.

"You are an Earthman," ran a thought in his mind. "The woman and the man are Klogorons."

Thor said eagerly, "You know that? Then you must also know where we are—how we came here?"

"I know, yes."

"And those men that come and go? And why we see no cities, no habitations where they live? Do you know that too?"

"The Discoverer knows everything. I am the Discoverer. I live everywhere and nowhere. Or at least I did until the madness that is this queer space lapped out at me and brought me here, just as it did you.

"To understand, you must think of the universe that you know as a big, big bubble. It is stable and steady. It has its star clusters with their space velocities and planetal orbits. Inside the big bubble everything is orderly—except one thing.

"That one thing is a very tiny bubble. A sort of cancer, you might say. It obeys no laws. Its very space coordinates and vectors are different than ours. It is fluid—always in motion. Its space segments are so alien that they can reach right through ordinary space, annihilating distance, and seize upon objects."

"But that's nonsensical," protested Thor.

The Discoverer thought-beamed, "I said it is not space as we know space. Let me put it this way: the magnet can draw metal to it without touching the metal. So this space-cancer can attract objects by reaching out for them, drawing them toward it—through a sort of purplish mist—by some power of magnetic attraction."

Thor made a sound as if he understood, and the Discoverer went on, "The segment of the rebel-universe came through the true universe, and touched you—"

"Touched my house on the Midwestern campus."

"Yes. It drew you within itself—"

"But Karola and Slag! They came out of the air right in the middle of my living room."

"They were in the magnetic pull, too. And where their space and this space met, was the middle of your living room."

Thor looked at Karola, whose forehead was wrinkled in tiny furrows as she followed the thoughts of the Discoverer. Slag was off to the right, chasing a fat rabbit bounding ahead of him in terror.

The Discoverer went on, "I sought entrance to this world many eons ago. It was one of the few spots in space I had never visited. Again and again I sought to enter, but its strangely twisted space-time continuum proved too much. Always I failed.

"And then, when I was visiting—I am almost all brain and it is a habit of mine to roam a bit—I was visiting a planet of what you call the Magellanic Cluster when everything went blank and I found myself tugged through the purple space and landed here, stretched across a rock."

Thor said, "You claim you can roam, mentally. Away from your body, that is."

"Your world would call it astral projection, in which the spirit levitates from the body and crosses distance. The high-energy potential of the mind is used to dissociate the ethereal self, with which I include the mental self, from the matter of the body."

Thor grunted dubiously, but the Discoverer went on, "I was engaged in astral projection to the Magellanic Cluster when this space lapped at my body that rested in the ruins of ancient Flormaseron. It is a form of magnetic current that did the trick. Not ordinary magnetism, but a current of it."

Thor thought of the Ehrenhaft experiments and nodded. He said, "And what of this world where we are? We saw some men—"

"Not men. Androids. They are semi-human, invested by Aava with a synthetic life force."

"Aava?"

"Aava is the Green Flame. He rules this land. He is like nothing I have ever seen. He can create, to an extent. He can destroy. He has made androids to serve him, but he is limited in materials on this planet. It is mostly rock and sand. If he had enough material, he could make millions of the androids. As it is, he can, and has made only thousands."

Thor said abruptly, "Can we get back to Earth and to Klogor?"

"Defeat Aava, learn the secret of this universe and destroy it, and you may return."

"Aava. You called him the Green Flame. Where can I find him?"

Thor caught a flicker of humor in the thoughts that flooded his brain. "Would you see Aava? I will show him to you. Lie down, on your back. So. I warn you, control your thoughts. If Aava suspects he is watched, you are doomed."

Karola pressed his arm against her warm side. Her violet eyes glared in fear out of the white, lovely face. Her scarlet mouth begged, "Do not do it, Thor. I beg you. I am afraid."

"There is nothing to fear. The Discoverer sounds as if he knows what he's doing. And you *do* want to go back to Klogor, don't you?"

The girl flushed so that a delicate pale rose flooded her neck and cheeks. Her violet eyes were brilliant as her torrent of gold hair seemed to gather new brightness from the sun.

"I am not sure. It is a nice life, this roaming in open air, across great prairies."

Thor held her hand. "You wait. I'll be back."

He lay down. His last recollection was the feel of Karola's long nails pressing the flesh of his hand...

THOR hung bodiless in blackness. He was aware with all the five senses of him, that life teemed about and all around the blackness, that something walked and spoke and moved. Thor struggled until a dull pain pounded and throbbed all through his being.

"Patient. Be patient," counseled a gentle voice.

"Are you the Discoverer?"

"I am he. It would be too dangerous to let you take your first mentastral flight alone. Besides, your brain has not the electrical potential sufficient to let you make progress. Hush, now. Listen!"

There were voices, deep and thunderous in a rolling wave of sound. Dim and faint at first, the paean swelled and pulsed. And as the sound grew, so came the light—

at first in tiny riplets of grayness that shimmered and fled—then a refulgent glory in broad bands.

He hung above the broad walls and ramparts of a queer city, whose domes and minarets were queerly bent and twisted. The broad avenues and narrow alleys were bare. It was a dead city.

"Not a dead city. Listen!" The song was louder, richer.

"Lower yourself. Think yourself down."

Thor found himself sweeping in a gentle arc closer and closer to the towers and temple domes. Now the song was crashing out in ponderous triumph.

"Go through the golden dome. You can do it."

Yellow metal shone and glimmered as he dropped gently through opalescent hues of gold and amber and yellow. It was like thick water, with faint bubbles glistening, locked within. He broke free and hung in the groined ceiling above a great chamber.

Hundreds of the androids with the glittering jewels on their chests stood arm to arm. Their rich voices boomed tribute toward a niche cut in the north wall, arched and wide, which held a squat black urn resting on a white alabaster pedestal.

"The song is nearly done. Watch the urn."

All sound and movement died away.

A tongue of green fire stabbed upwards out of the black urn. For one long instant it hung there, quivering and pulsing. It broke and faded into green mist that the breezes blew out across the chamber.

"That was the manifestation of Aava. Now we will see him as he really is."

They swept through the air with the speed of light. Matter that was wall and stone and metal blurred into a liquescent dimness that darkened the further they went. From gray to black to grim jet went the colors. And still they went on. Now the color grew light tan, like sand.

"We are in the bowels of the Mountains of Distortion. The blackness is rock hidden forever from a glimpse of sunlight. We are nearly there. Go cautiously! This buried desert is right above him."

It was a cave. From the high rock ceiling stalactites drooped like the fringes of a weeping willow eternally etched in stone. Amid a riotous profusion of club shaped stalagmites thrusting up from the rough cave floor, lay a circle of red space.

And in the red space stood Aava.

Green light, flickering and flaring, now subdued, now pouring forth in a verdant shower of pride and strength, flooded the cave. Thor could feel its sentience through every beat and pulse of it. Like the tongue of some mighty star trapped in matter, it licked and thrust and strove to speak its greatness.

The green fire lowered, hung brooding. "I smell men."

"Careful," thought the Discoverer. Thor moved no muscle, took no breath in his spirit form. Yet the machinations of his mind slipped a cog. He thought, and the green flames knew.

A sword of flame lunged outward, at him. He felt its heat, the wild life of it, the pride and all the cruelty.

He tried to cry out. Then his mind went. The last he knew was the voice of the Discoverer.

"Come!"

THOR gasped lungfuls of sweet, cool air, staring up at the sun in the blue sky. Yellow hair splashed on his face and chest as Karola wept and whimpered. Wonderingly, Thor put a big hand to his face. It was beaded with damp sweat.

The Discoverer beamed a thought at him.

"That was a near thing, man of Earth. Had I not kept constant control of your mind, Aava would have had you."

"What—what is he? That green fire is alive. I could feel it. I knew its emotions."

"Aava is alive. He has been alive for eons piled upon eons. His beginning I know not. Whether he will have an end—I also know not."

Thor shuddered.

The Discoverer went on, "Destroy Aava, and destroy his universe, and you may return to your own. But how can you destroy Aava when even I, the Discoverer, must admit failure?"

Thor shook his head. Destroy that flame? It was impossible.

When he looked up, the Discoverer was oozing a path into the distance and Karola was hugging herself to him. Thor put an arm around her, smiling grimly into her frightened eyes.

"We're in it, baby. All the way. Lost in some mad corner of space that nobody can get in or out of. Trapped. And me with an education to catch up on. Although," he grinned, looking at her thick yellow hair and large red mouth, "I'm not feeling any too scholarly at the moment. Yeah, I guess it could be worse. I guess it could."

Slag came toward them with three rabbits dangling from his right hand. He knelt and began to make a fire. Thor and Karola watched him until the roasting flesh scents reached their nostrils.

Thor laughed, "Hell. I'm just hungry. After a good meal, I'll feel better about it all."

But that meal was never finished.

The androids came in the middle of the second rabbit. One moment there were only the stars and the rolling meadowland, and the red flames making shadows on the grass and on their arms and legs. The next they were falling out of thin air, all over them, fists hitting at Slag and Thor, hands reaching out for, and lifting, a screaming, clawing Karola.

"Thor! Thor!" she cried.

Thor heaved up from under three androids. His muscles rended with the strain, but he threw them from him. His fists lashed out and thudded into rib and jaw. He clove a path through living men, dropping them with chops and uppercuts.

Karola stood writhing in the grasp of three giants. Their hands were wrapped about her wrists, and their free hands fumbled at the jewels that hung about their necks.

Thor flung an android from him; whirled to his left, avoiding a sword thrust, hitting down with the edge of his hand against the android's neck even as he turned. His knees slid under another's knife and splintered his ribs. He heard Slag's club crunching home to his left, but all he could see was Karola with the firelight playing across legs and midriff.

"Thor! Thor! It's dark, Thor! I'm frightened!"

Her scream sent cold horror into his spine. Her white feet were almost in the fire. How could it be dark to her? Unless these fiends who came and went were blinding her—

Thor roared.

He lowered his head and charged, as some Viking ancestor might have charged a longboat's deck. His fists hammered and clubbed. He blasted a path through cursing, sobbing men.

Karola was in front of him.

He reached out for her.

Karola disappeared.

Thor felt his hands sink through empty space where Karola should have been; where she was standing, one instant before. On straddled legs he stood, naked chest gulping in cool air, staring at the darkness.

"Karola!" he cried.

The androids were all fading. Thor dimly understood that it was Karola they had been after, seeing them drop into nothingness, one after the other. The fire flared brighter. In its red beams, one still sat, fumbling a little dazedly at the jewel on his chest. Thor knew his own thoughts were fumbling, just as the other's fingers were. Karola was gone. The androids were going, only one was left. There was no way to follow.

The firelight hung in the ruby jewel for one bursting moment, like red blood bursting. Red jewel. Fumbling fingers clawing at it. Three androids with Karola also clawing at their jewels. And Karola disappearing—

Thor leaped.

His big right hand stabbed for the ruby. He closed his fingers on it and tugged. The chain resisted, and then the android came awake to what Thor wanted and pounded at him. Thor lowered his head and chin until his jaw rested against his chest and hunched his shoulders. He rode the buffets, swaying as he did in the ring.

Tug, tug. Tug and tear with that right hand, his mind kept telling him.

Get that jewel!

It broke and came loose in his hand. The android screamed, reaching out. Slag came over the fire with a tremendous bound and his club swung. It caved in the android's head and toppled him forward into the fire.

Thor stared at the dying green fire that spilled from the android's head. That was a part of Aava, that fire. It was the life force.

He looked at the jewel throbbing soft red fire in his palm. He grinned.

CHAPTER TWO

THE RUBY WAS THE SIZE OF A small egg. It was cut and polished until its burnished sides threatened to obscure the inner fires with their glimmerings. But deep inside the jewel was a core of flame that would never be extinguished. That flame looked purple.

Thor wondered. Purple heart of red ruby. Suppose Aava had imprisoned a jot of his immortal fire inside the ruby, as he had with the androids!

He turned it over. There was a rocking instant of vertigo, of pitch-blackness and cold.

The meadowlands were gone. He was standing on a rocky escarpment that brooded over a small valley. And set in the middle of the valley, like a vision from an Arabic nightmare, was a city of elfin loveliness. Towers pointed slender spires to the sky, and hemispheric domes glowed softly in pale moonlight.

"The City of Aava," murmured Thor. "This is the place they sang the song to the urn, the city the Discoverer showed me."

His fingers tightened on the ruby. He turned it carefully.

He was back with Slag.

The dwarf-man was whining, and looking around him like a scared dog until he saw Thor looming massive in the fire flames. He grinned and came close, shaking his club.

"You go where Karola went? Where the men come from?"

"Yes. It's a different world, Slag, but the same. I've a feeling this ruby with the green fire in it is some sort of passport, or key, that unlocks the path into Aava's realm. It's a physical manifestation of a geometry Euclid never got around to. Dimensional worlds."

Slag grunted. "We go after her?"

"Take hold of the ruby. That's it."

Their hands held the warm jewel. Slowly they turned it. Darkness and coldness, and dizziness, and Slag and Thor found rock under their feet, and a white moon high above them.

Thor hunted for and found a narrow path of rock that twisted from the escarpment and curved downwards toward the valley. He called to Slag and they trotted Indian fashion along it.

The walls of the elfin city loomed gigantic as they crossed the sandy plain that stretched for miles in front of it. Cyclopean stones were fitted one on another until they spread up and up, seemingly toward the stars themselves. Thor felt like a midge about to attack a mastodon.

His feet kicked endless grains of dust walking along that massive barrier. Mile after mile they trudged, and found no gates.

Slag said, "How get in?"

Thor put a hand in his frayed pocket and drew out the warm ruby. He said, "This must be the only key. We haven't found any door yet."

They put hands on the jewel and moved it. They went forward over the red grasslands for a hundred feet.

Thor said. "This ought to be just about right." Once more they turned the jewel, and experienced the dark, the coldness, and the vertigo.

Cobblestones underfoot, and smooth rock walls lining the streets as they crept forward. It was a dead city lying under the white moon, stark in its emptiness, sorrowful in its brooding strength. The windows were dark, the doorways shadowed.

Once Thor and Slag heard footsteps, but they came from a great distance, and soon faded into the eternal silence.

Ahead of them loomed the temple with the golden dome, where the paean to Aava had thundered forth, where the urn that held the green flame stood on its white pedestal.

"They will have taken Karola there, to Aava," whispered Thor. "That is where we must go. To the temple of the green flame."

A massive knob of bronze, covered with greenish rot and carved with the emblem of Aava-in-the-urn, screeched as Thor turned it. The thick oaken door swung wide. Pale radiance bathed the arched columns that trod the mosaic floor of the vast chamber. At the far end of the room, the black urn stood empty and black.

Thor ran across the vast chamber, his footfalls sounding loud and lonely. He stepped to the white pedestal and peered within the black urn. Green flakes and crystal chips encrusted the bowled bottom of the urn.

He slipped a torn handkerchief from his pocket, and with the buckle of his belt, loosened some of the crystal chips.

"I don't know whether I can ever analyze these," he said to Slag, "but I'll take them along, anyhow."

Slag stood at one of the tall, arched windows, red head gleaming in the sun. He was making guttural noises in his throat, and he kept lifting and dropping his big war club. Thor stepped to his side and looked into the streets.

Men were walking stealthily along the cobblestones.

THOR blinked and rubbed his eyes. He was staring down at men clad in chain-mail armor, men in fur skins, men in suits of the same cut as he wore. There was a huge creature that Thor would have sworn was an ape, except for the two tusks depending from its lips, and its erect, intelligent bearing. There was a four-legged being, and something that had two heads. There was—

"They are men, Slag. Real men. Not androids!"

He felt a warm delight in him, a welling of friendliness inspired by the weeks of wandering on the red, lonely grasslands. He lifted an arm and opened his lips to shout. A mental censor made him close his mouth. It would be better to wait, to see what manner of men these were who stalked the empty streets of a deserted city, before showing himself.

Thor vaulted over the stone sill, calling to Slag to follow. Side by side they crept after the group.

They went deeper into the heart of the city. By twisted alleys the stalkers went, and their furtive tread and cautious glances told Thor that they were in hostile territory. Where a building cast gloomy shadows, he ran nearer, until he could distinguish voices.

To his amazement, some of the beings spoke English. He could catch fragments of words, of phrases. Mixed with his own language were terms of the jewel-speech of Klogor. And there were other tongues, too, languages that were like the cacklings of monkeys or the shrill treble of singing birds. They were mingled together, as through the ages of common living had created a new tongue that was all of none, yet something of each.

Thor whispered to Slag, "They are after women."

"So are we, Karola."

"Yes. I wonder now—"

He stood out from the shadows and called, "I am an American."

A man in tweed suit that hung in tatters from bulky shoulders whirled and stared. His hair was pale blond, and his eyes were icy blue. Thor didn't need his, "Jove, you are!" to tell he was from England.

"Thor Masterson," he said, putting out a hand.

The Englishman chuckled. "Peter Gordon. I'm a gentleman farmer—or was, you know—from Devon. When did you get into this place?"

"A few weeks ago. How long've you been here?"

"Seven years, near as I can make it. How—how are things back—back there?"

Thor told him. Gordon opened wide eyes at news of the war. He shook his head, smiling. "It seems so far away, when you've lived here for a while. It's as though you knew no other life, Jove! War. Well, we fight a war here all the time. With the Black Priest. He and his men raid our little settlements. For women, you know. Have to raid back, naturally. Got to have women to breed kids to fight the Flame."

Gordon led Thor forward toward a group of three. One was the white-haired ape. When Thor looked into his eyes, he saw keen intelligence blazing out of black eyes. Another was a lavender-tinted man clad in broad leathern belt and kilt of dark maroon. He was from a planet named Zarathza. The third man was a giant in a black fur mantle, who carried a spear that looked like a small Oregon pine.

"We must attack that low-walled building over there," said the Zarathzan, whose name was Tor Kan. "They keep the women in there. We don't have many weapons, as you can see. We'll lose a lot of men."

Thor thought of the robots he had fought. They didn't seem like such brilliant warriors. He said so.

The giant in the black fur grunted, "A frontal attack is always costly, even if you fought against women."

"Why attack frontally? Create a diversion, with a false attack, then slip through the walls—"

"Through the walls? You sound like a bally ghost," smiled Gordon.

Thor lifted the ruby from his pocket and showed it to them. Their eyes bulged in awe, looking at it. "A gatestone!" whispered the Zarathzan, licking his lips. "With that we could go anywhere."

The white ape, whom Thor later learned was from Fomalhaut's fifth planet and called Yorg, drew back his lips from his big fangs. He rumbled, "Let the American hasten himself and his red dwarf through the walls with a few of us. Others will storm the gates of the compound. The American can open the gates when he is inside. If," he added wistfully, "he could get us a few of the robots' weapons—"

Thor grinned. "Come on, Yorg. You and Slag and I will turn ourselves into an ordnance crew. We'll get the weapons."

They joined hands and turned the ruby.

The red grasslands were back, blowing in the breeze. The three ran swiftly forward. Yorg, who knew the compound almost as he did his own settlement, called to them to halt.

"Now turn the gatestone."

When the blackness of the dimensional barrier faded, Thor found himself in a room that was formed by a circle of gray stones. From wooden racks inset in the stone hung swords and spears, tall bows and metal-tipped arrows.

Yorg whispered, "There is almost no metal on this planet. That partially accounts for the reason that we fight with bows and arrows. To make weapons that are any more powerful you need steel and other iron alloys. And besides, I often think that Aava only trusts his androids as far as he can see them.

"The magnetic current of the planet that drags men and women and anything it touches onto its surface must at some time or other have taken potent weapons. But if there are any, only Aava knows where they are hidden. Then too, you need intelligence to use complicated weapons. The androids possess only a pseudo-intellect."

Trip after trip the trio made, their heavily muscled arms laden with every weapon in the arsenal. Once Yorg said grimly, "If ever we had a gatestone in our possession before, things would be different today." He looked at Thor and added, "The man who owns a gatestone could rule the settlements."

"I don't want to rule anything," growled Thor. "I just want to find my woman—and have another go at Aava."

YORG had been slashing air with a sword, testing its balance. Now he lowered the point and popped black eyes at Thor, in amazement. "Another go? Have you seen Aava? And you live?"

As they carted the weapons back across the grasslands, Thor told him of his experience with the Discoverer. York listened in silence, then dropped a gigantic paw to his naked shoulder.

"Forget Aava," he counseled. "Aava is too powerful. Nothing can defeat him."

"I'm a funny guy," replied Thor. "The longer the odds, the better I fight. It's a sort of tradition in my country. The Alamo. Custer and his last stand. Bataan, Wake Island. Yeah, I'd like another try at Aava. Some of these days, I'll get around to it."

Tor Kan crooned in his throat when he fitted his palm around the hilt of a sword. Morlon, the giant in the black fur pulled his lips back from white teeth in delight as he hefted a huge bow. Peter Gordon twanged a bowstring, with, "I used to do a bit of archery in Devon. For fun, you know. I haven't forgotten how to feather a shaft."

In the shadows, the other weapons were handed out to eager hands while throats whined in battle lust.

They turned to Thor then, and stood waiting. He drew a deep breath. "The best archers among you, do you know them? Good. You're the artillery. You stand in the shadows and shoot at any who show themselves on that wall. You others—swordsmen and spearmen— follow Tor Kan and Yorg. They'll charge for the gates. Slag and I will get inside the compound walls and open them for you.

"Listen, all of you. Listen well.

"I don't know whether any of us will ever go back to what we used to call home. Maybe there isn't any need for that. We have a world all our own, now. We can make it what we will.

"But we have to defeat Aava. Don't flinch at his name. He has you licked already if you do that. By fighting his robots, you're fighting him. They're his arms and legs. Take them away and Aava isn't anything!"

Their voices growled angry reassurances in the shadows. Weapons glinted as they were swung, shimmery in the moon rays.

"Come, Slag."

The purple light deep inside the ruby seemed to flare in mad anger as Thor held the jewel in his palm, looking down at it. Turn it slowly, turn it gently. Go into the darkness and the nothingness, to—

Thor stood inside the walls. Ahead of him was the great gate with rusted bolt, looming in the white walls like a gap between bright teeth. He leaped for the bolt and wrenched at it.

Slag came to help him. Between them they broke the rust of years, watching reddish flakes fly as the barrel-bolt turned in its groove.

An arrow plunked into the wooden door, an inch from Thor's brown hair where it hung to his big shoulders. He whirled and deflected its fellow with his sword as Slag threw wide the gates.

A horde of furred and savage fighters came roaring into the compound, swords and war clubs in their hands. Thor saw the androids swarming from the far side of the enclosure, racing to meet the invaders. Yorg grasped his arm and swung him around.

"The women," he gasped. "Hurry! We won't have much time. Those androids can only be stopped by smashing the machinery inside their skulls."

Thor ran with the white ape across the hard flooring of the pavilion. He could hear the screams and excited cries of women beyond the inner battlements.

He hit the lock a blow that crumpled the cup-guard of his blade, but the lock broke. Yorg threw open the doors.

"Come! All you women, come!"

Thor pressed against the open gate, staring at women in rags, women naked, women in torn silks and satins. There were red heads, and brunettes, and girls with hair the color of old amber. Some were lovely, some ugly, some were furred like Yorg. They ran silently, scenting freedom.

Thor was a tall man. Standing, he looked over those tossing heads, seeking Karola. He saw her in the press, clothes almost ripped entirely away. He bellowed and shook his battered sword above his head.

He clove a path to her, swung her up on his hip, and ran.

She whimpered, "It is glorious, but useless—*look!*"

Thor stared toward a balcony four feet above the sun-baked floor of the compound. A giant of an android, with bristling black beard matting his red face was gesturing to three others who were bent and straining at something between them.

When they moved, Thor saw it was the black urn.

"It is Aava," Karola whispered hoarsely," The women told me of him. And that is the Black Priest, the one they call Malgrim. He will move the urn to face us. Aava will kill all, even his own men. What are men to Aava?"

A scream of fear and fury tore from the throats of the fighters. Shrilling above it was the frightened cry of the women.

Yorg was bellowing, "The gates! Fly! Save yourselves, if you can."

It was too late. The urn was turning in the hands of the androids.

THE Black Priest cried in a strangely sweet voice for such a man, "Foolish rebels! For the last time you have dared defy the power of all-consuming Aava. This time you die! Swing the urn. Let the outlaws taste the green kiss of mighty Aava, that he may take them with him to the land of nevermore!"

The black orifice of the urn was becoming rounder as it tilted down. Deep in the rounded bowl, green fire shimmered. Thor went forward, swinging his sword. It was not as good as an axe, but it would do. He flung it straight for the broad chest of the Black Priest, and followed it.

He saw the blade go deep into the man, saw him stagger backwards, bellowing his rage. Then Thor was reaching for the top rail of the balcony, leaping, his legs like springs beneath him.

Thor caught the top rail and used it as the pole-vaulter uses his pole. His wrists turned and his hips twisted. He went up over the bar.

His feet hit the urn, with two hundred pounds of muscles and desperation behind it.

The urn tilted back.

The androids screamed as the green flame leaped outward. For one instant they hung there, as though in green mist. Their open mouths and bulging eyes were straining to escape what they tasted and saw. It was no use.

Thor knew the androids were dissolving even as he brought his left fist up to the Black Priest's jaw. The man went back, heels dragging on the balcony floor. He lay where he had fallen, motionless.

Thor went and stared into the urn. The green flame was dead, now, just glittering green stuff, like crystallized moss.

Yorg called, "Hurry, Thor Masterson. We have broken them but Aava will send more."

He swung from the balcony, a frown furrowing his forehead. There was something about that green flame—

Karola was waiting for him. She slipped her hand in his and tugged. "We mustn't stay here, Thor. You heard what Yorg said."

Thor stepped over fallen androids, with arrows and lances jutting from mouth and eye-sockets, with crushed and split-open skulls.

Thor stood in the arch of the gates and stared back at the balcony where the black urn lay tilted. That green stuff! His head was churning, trying to catch the elusive thought that dipped and darted out of reach of his mental hands. He shook his head.

"There's something about Aava—"

"Thor, please. There isn't time. Yorg says at any moment Aava will send androids to surround us. They will fetch other urns. We will die."

He snapped awake to the knowledge that he was walking with a frightened Karola behind the others, that ahead of him the women and the men were running. They had gone through the gates and were spreading out over the streets and alleys of the cyclopean city.

"Yorg! Tor Kan! Gordon!"

The Englishman heard him, came to him through the press, his longbow strung with a ready arrow.

"Jolly brush, what? Found I haven't lost my eye for a target. Got thirty of the blighters, myself."

Thor said, "We'll never escape Aava in his city. There's only one chance. We have to use the gatestone, and scatter. Can you get the others?"

Peter threw back his head and sent a shrill cry ululating across the streets. The men and women paused, looking back over their shoulders. Gordon waved an arm. Fearfully, the listeners began to return.

Thor lifted out the ruby, told the others to grasp it, as many as possible. He said.

"Once we get into that other world, it will be easy for us to lose ourselves. Aava and his Black Priest do not know we possess a gatestone. They will search for us here in the city. While they hunt here, we will be far away."

Kor Tan rumbled, "Good. We will find our way as close as possible to our settlements. Then you, Thor Masterson, will find us with that ruby."

Hands stretched out. The ruby turned.

IT DID NOT take long. A ruby will turn swiftly in a steady hand, making many trips with people eager to be saved from the green blast of Aava. There were some who had not heard Peter Gordon call, and they stayed behind in the city. But the great majority of them were taken through the dimensional door by the red ruby, and set down on waving grasslands and bleak rocks.

With the red grasses brushing his ankles, Thor said, "We cannot search for the others. Aava will have his androids in the streets. Scatter now. Make your way toward the settlement. Gordon, will you come with us? I don't know my way to the settlement of yours."

"Glad to, Masterson."

Slag, Karola, Thor and the Englishman watched the others walk swiftly to the four corners of the horizon.

Gordon said, "We'd better take the most roundabout way I can think of. It will take us longer, but it will be safer. You have the gatestone. No one must get you."

They travelled swiftly and lightly for four days. Peter Gordon brought down juicy rabbits with his arrows for food, and taught Slag to use his weapon. With the wild man's aptitude for arms, the red dwarf was swift to learn.

On the morning of the fifth day, Thor Masterson went ahead of the others to scout. He strode up over massive rocks, to reach the summit of a small hill from which to look into the next valley.

When he reached the top, he halted in amazement.

A SHIP rested on black rock, tilted over. On the rotted white sail, there were the remnants of a dragon's head worked in red. From the prow, with its up reared serpent's neck and gaping jaws and forked tongue, to the stern where a broken rudder lay across the rock, it was every inch a Viking ship. A few shields still hung on the wooden sides. The mast, splintered, stood at a dangerous angle from the sloping deck.

Thor went up the rudder-stick and clambered over the side.

A skeleton lay near the helm, a vest of rusted-through chain-mail pooled on the white bones. A little in front of what had been a hand, lay a great axe.

Thor grinned, seeing that axe. He reached for the ivory haft, lifted and swung it around his head.

He staggered.

The pain was unbearable, there in his side. He reached down, felt in his pocket. His fingers closed on the ruby.

With a curse, he flung the jewel from him. His palm still stung from its icy coldness. The ruby hit the deck and bounded across the ancient planks. It rolled to a stop near a shield.

Thor stared at it.

The ruby was changing, right there, in front of him. It pulsed and throbbed with the light inside it. Its red hues gave way to deep, royal purple—an angry purple.

Thor went nearer. He could see the beat and heave of the Green Flame, trapped in the crystallized alumina. It waxed and surged, as though battering against its jeweled walls.

"Aava!" he whispered.

"Of course, Aava. Did you think I put parts of my immortal self in these bits of stuff to pass the time? They are myself; I, them. It is my method of keeping watch on all on my planet. I am with every android who carries a gatestone, if I so will."

Thor lifted the axe; he looked from it to the ruby, at the greenish fire flaring within it.

"No use," Aava thought-waved at him. "You cannot harm me, just as I cannot harm you—in this form. I have been searching for you. You invaded the Cave of Life with the Discoverer. You stole a gatestone. You raided my arsenal and woman-stockade. You assaulted the Black Priest. You overturned Aava in the urn. A long list for one man."

There was silence. Above his head, Thor heard the rotting sail flap dismally in the slight wind. He shifted and a plank creaked underfoot.

Aava went on, "But I am a patient being, and kind. I bear no ill will. Become my man, you who call yourself—what is it—Thor? You will not regret your move."

Thor thought of Karola's golden hair and red mouth, of Peter Gordon and his bow, of Slag, of Kor Tan, of white Yorg. They and the others were depending upon him. They needed him and his gates tone to return them to their settlements and safety and peace.

He shook his head, gripping the war-axe tighter.

Aava chuckled. "You *are* an idiot, aren't you? Oh, I can read your thoughts. It isn't hard for someone who's spent an untold eternity of eons living by one's self. You train yourself to do things... You have loyalty in your heart. You love this woman with the yellow hair.

"But what is one woman? What are casual friends? I can give you more than that. I can give you anything you want.

"Permit me to demonstrate. Turn the gatestone."

The sail flapped louder in the breeze. A shaft of sunlight glinted on the edge of a shield fastened to the side of the longboat. Thor bit his tongue inside his mouth. It came home to him suddenly, with the force of a powerfully swung sledge, that he was trapped irrevocably.

The outlaws who fought Aava needed the gatestone to get to their settlements. He had the gatestone, but Aava was alive and awake, inside it. Whenever and wherever he used it, Aava would know. The settlements would no longer be secret. If he used the gatestone to transport the outlaws home, he would be leading an army to slay them!

Thor growled in his throat.

Aava laughed softly. He urged, "Turn the gatestone. Let me show you the wonders I could give a man like you, were he to be my friend. I want a friend, a strong friend. I do not trust my androids overly. They are only pseudo-life. Besides, there are too few of them to build an empire with. Lack of materials to make them has hampered me.

"Will you be my friend, Thor?"

Thor blinked. The insidiously sweet voice was working its will on him. He found himself thinking about those wonders and those marvels. Why not? What allegiance did he owe Gordon and the rest? Karola now, that was different. And Slag.

"You may have your woman, if you want her after I show you—my brand of woman!"

"It is a trick!" Thor rasped.

"What trick? What harm can I do you inside this jewel?"

That was true enough. If worst came to worst, he could always stuff the ruby into his pocket and get away. Aava couldn't see where he was going inside a dark pocket. He could see only when he was out in the open, such as he would be when Thor used the ruby as a gatestone.

"Use it, man."

Thor bent and held out his hand toward the red gem. It winked and flirted with him with its gorgeous purple hues. It was no longer cold with the iciness that stung. It was warm, with the heat of a human body. His fingers closed on it. The ruby throbbed softly, like a living heart.

"Now—turn me!"

GONE was the ship with its flapping sail and ancient planking. Gone was the sea of grass and the broken rocks. Thor almost dropped the ruby, staring.

A fey city stood not one hundred feet from him, set on the hard sands. It glowed with the creamy luminescence of alabaster where sunshafts struck its white walls and domes and needled spires. Crimson

166

bands, interlaced with black, formed patterns of eerie loveliness against the whiteness. Inside its walls a chorus of sweet voices chanted with ensorcelled harmony.

The red doors in the wall swung open.

Chariots drawn by great black stallions raced toward him. Standing behind the hooped fronts were women of exquisite loveliness, their hair streaming behind them, whips held in red-nailed hands. They sang as they came, a song of sounds that stirred the senses.

"This is yours, Thor. All yours."

"It is unreal. It is too lovely to be real."

"It is real."

The lead chariot slithered on the sands, powdering Thor's ankles with grit. The black stallions reared, their hooves slashing at air.

The girl in the chariot caught Thor's eyes with hers, and laughed. She tossed the reins aside and stepped from the tailboard. Her red hair hung to her waist in back, and was powdered with silver dust. She held out white hands to Thor.

Thor reached out and grasped her hands. They felt real. And looking into her brown eyes, seeing all the beauty of her in gauze skirt and white linen cloak worked with a border of red and black interlacing, he almost felt his doubts vanish.

His fingers rubbed at her hand, twisting the flesh. That was real flesh. The girl seemed to catch his thought, for she came nearer and pressed herself to him.

"Kiss me, and know," she breathed.

Her mouth was warm and clinging. After a while she drew away and laughed. "Well?"

"You're real."

Aava whispered, "All yours, Thor. Go with her. Let her show you the city that, is yours, that belongs to the friend of Aava."

He thought of Karola waiting with Slag and Peter Gordon. He felt the warm hand of the red-haired girl tug him. Her red mouth blew him a kiss. Her voice murmured cloyingly, "Come, Thor. Come to your city, and your throne." Karola seemed far away, forgotten.

Behind the black stallions, the chariot swept on toward the city. It rode smoothly, easily over the sun-baked sands. The red walls came nearer, nearer. Now he was under them, and inside the city.

Balconies on either side of the broad avenue were hung with banners and rich draperies. Men and women in red and yellow and purple garments laughed and tossed flowers at him, on the backs of the horses, into the street before him.

"Thor! Lord Thor!" they cried with delight in their voices, and awe and worship in their eyes.

The girl leaned into the hook of his arm. She said, "This is your city, Lord Thor. These are your people."

He looked into her brown eyes.

"And you?"

She put her mouth to his and left it there while the chariot thundered over roses and carnations and the pavement of the streets. Later she whispered, "Stalyl is yours, too." And Thor rode with chin held high, and pride in the set of his shoulders.

Before great doors of carved quartz the chariots came to a stop. Stalyl walked with Thor between the doors, her hip brushing his, her fingers wrapped around his fingers.

Alabaster pillars rose from an alabaster floor toward a red alabaster ceiling. Sunlight poured molten pools on the floor through tall windows. At the far end of the massive hall, on an oval dais of iridescent opal, stood a gigantic jewel, carved in the semblance of a throne.

"Lord Thor—your throne," said Stalyl softly.

He went and sat on the cold edge of the massy carnelian, fingering scarlet arms. In front of him, Stalyl clapped her hands, and young girls garbed in trousers of striped satin led giant men by chains around their necks. The men bore caskets in their hands.

Girls and men knelt before the throne. The caskets were placed in an arc before Thor.

Stalyl went to the first casket, threw back the cover.

Thor choked. It was filled to the brim with diamonds, diamonds that shimmered and glittered in the sunlight. Stepping down, he reached out a hand and dipped it into the jewels. He bore a handful, staring at them. Cut and polished with expert care, the diamonds were white fire against his palm.

Aava spoke, casting a thought at him from the depths of his pocket, "You like what I have prepared for my friend, Lord Thor?"

Thor drew out the ruby and held it free in his palm, staring from ruby to diamonds. "This is my price, eh, Aava? I sell my friends for these jewels?"

The purple hues of the ruby grew cloudy, as though with hurt. "Who spoke of selling your friends? I ask no traitor to come to me. I want the friendship of a true man."

Stalyl moved closer, touching his arm. Her red hair was a flaming halo around the white, red-lipped face.

Her brown eyes burned at him. She was a living witch's spell of beauty and desire. Her nearness made Thor tremble.

He opened one hand, and diamonds tinkled on the mosaic floor. He reached out for the girl, seeing her lips beckon.

The ruby flared warmer, hot with pride. It dragged Thor back to reality, drumming alarums into his core. Danger, danger! With a wrench he tore his gaze from Stalyl; looked at the ruby, saw the green fire beating up with delight.

Thor tottered.

He knew, now. Somehow. In some strange manner—

Aava had triumphed!

CHAPTER THREE

THE ROTTING SAIL FLAPPED and bellied over his head. He stood again on the longboat deck. Out there, all around him, was the red grassland. Gone was the city of alabaster and the red witch, Stalyl. A myth. A hallucination. A mirage of temptation.

In their place—

Androids!

Thor drew his lips back from his teeth and flung the ruby from him. But as it twisted in air Aava cried, "A trick, Thor. But just a trick to test you. Pay no heed to the androids. They are here to lead us back to the city of the Urn. I tell you—" Thor caught his war-axe where it rested against the helm. He shook it at the ruby.

"You foul liar!" he rasped. "You hypnotized me. You showed me things that existed only in your mind. All right. I'll play your little game. But I'll show you things, too. And the things I show you will be real. Real, like death, Aava!

"You don't know what death is, do you? But you'll learn. I'll find a way. I'll pay you back—"

A lance sang in the air as it slid over his head. The androids were closer, hemming him in. They began to clamber up the sides of the ship.

Aava said, swiftly, "You can make the dream come true, Thor! With you to help, I shall build a city of alabaster, make it lovely as the one I showed you.

"And Stalyl! We will create her, you and I. We will make her as lovely as the Stalyl I showed you. Far lovelier than any woman—"

"You lack materials! Otherwise you would have made more androids to fight the outlaws!"

An android hurdled the rail. Thor stepped forward, swung his axe. The keen edge bit through hair and skull.

Thor grunted, "This is the opening move, Aava. I'll find a gambit to beat you. I'll checkmate you yet."

The axe bit and dug at climbing androids, toppling them. Thor aimed always at the heads, for that was swift annihilation. Android after android dropped under the slashing impact of the double-edged Viking weapon. Thor used it with a full swing, letting the weight of his body add the impetus, learning that the perfect balance of the axe was manageable with a twist of the wrist. His hand on the ivory haft changed course and the edge drove home; it swerved, and the axe dipped under a sword to cut upwards through a jaw.

He spoke no more to Aava, though he felt the blazing green gaze fastened on him where he held the Viking deck. He used his wits for fighting.

After a while Thor dropped the tip of the axe to the deck and grinned at Aava. "You didn't send enough androids. Take a look!"

He held the ruby at arm's length above his head. The deck and sides of the ship were littered with sprawled bodies, with broken springs and gears spilling from crushed and severed heads.

Aava sighed. "It is hard, using androids. They are good servants, but they lack one thing. They lack initiative. They can't think."

Thor brought the ruby down, grinning mirthlessly into its depths. "How long have you lived, Aava?"

"I am immortal. I always was."

"You will die, some day. I will kill you, myself."

"Nothing can kill me, Thor."

"I will."

"Nothing can kill—"

Aava checked. Thor felt the cunning of the green fire, beating up through the crystal layers of the jewel. He whispered, "Nothing can kill—*what!* What are you, Aava? What is your secret?"

"You will never learn."

Thor shrugged and knelt. With his fingers he pried up a rotting board. There was a beam-joint beneath it. Thor placed the ruby in the crotch of the joint and stared down at the jewel, knowing the wild rage of Aava.

"I must leave you here—in darkness, Aava. I can't take you with me. If I did, you would see all I am going to do to whip you. You understand that?"

"Thor, be my friend!"

He shook his head. "I cannot. I do not trust you, Aava."

"The androids were not to fight you—"

"Yet they did."

Thor checked, peered closer. The purple hue of the ruby was fading. The gem was tenantless. Aava was gone.

Thor stood up and kicked the plank into place. He filled his lungs with crisp air. He knew what he must do. He had to learn all he could about Aava. If Gordon and the others could not help him—

There was always the Discoverer!

Thor dropped over the longboat side and went striding off into the grasslands.

IT WAS NIGHT when he found the campfire. Karola came running, hearing his shout, her yellow hair streaming behind her. Thor caught her, held her close. He thought of Stalyl, and there was remorse and tenderness in his kiss.

She felt his mood. Head tilted, she looked at him and whispered, "What is it? Where did you get that axe? And your eyes—there is a little sorrow in them. Why, Thor?"

"I will tell you, darling. But I must tell the others, too. I want Gordon's advice."

Gordon wrung his hand and then held out some cooked meat on the point of a sword. Thor was famished. He sat with legs crossed before him and ate and ate. Karola sat close to him, watching him with her large violet eyes. Once in a while she touched the great war axe, running the pink tips of her fingers along the fresh scratches on the steel.

Thor dug his greasy fingers into the sand, powdering them; then he rubbed them dry.

"I talked to Aava," he said slowly. "He came into the gatestone that I carried. He tempted me. I—almost yielded."

The others stared at him. Thor fastened his eyes on the heart of the fire, where the twigs and dried grasses glowed bright red. It was easier, looking there, to tell his tale, than to look into the eyes of his friends.

HE concluded, "I do not have the gatestone now. I left it there, in the ship. Otherwise, we would have Aava with us, with every move we make. And Aava is what we are fighting. The odds are bad enough, without taking your enemy into your confidence."

Thor raised his eyes. He looked at Karola. He said, "I am sorry. Say that it's all right."

To his surprise, she laughed. Her violet eyes poked fun at him. She whispered, "No woman can compete with a dream. Stalyl was only that. At the same time, a dream cannot compete with a living woman. I am a living woman." She leaned over and kissed him gently, then sat back.

Peter Gordon said slowly, "What can we do now? It's a rotten situation. The others expect us. If we can't find a way to return them to the settlement—" He broke off, shaking his head.

Thor slid his hand up and down the stained ivory haft of the axe. He said, "The androids came into this dimension with the use of a gatestone. If we could find it, we could use that one. All the robots were killed, but I saw no gatestone."

"Perhaps the Black Priest used one to transmit them into this world. Then there wouldn't be any gatestone at all," said Gordon.

Thor opened his eyes, and blinked. He got to his feet, lifting his axe. "There's a chance. Aava will send someone to get the gatestone I hid in the ship. Then, if he should return to the gatestone—or we can get us one from an android—there might be a chance."

Peter Gordon drew his bow toward him and strung it. "Let's go," he said gruffly.

They went in the dark of the night, when the moons were below the horizon. Thor led, trotting swiftly with the long Indian stride an old Cherokee had taught him. Karola and Slag ran side by side. Peter Gordon, bow in hand and fingers touching the string of it, loped far behind, eyes continually moving.

Hour after hour they ran. Over rolling grassland, with only an occasional clump of rock formation to break the barren monotony of the dark landscape, they went at a deceptive pace.

Thor almost went by the ship. It was easy to lose trail here, where no trees ever grew. But the moons were sweeping up, and in their light a shield-boss winked to the left. It was enough. Thor swung about and when he grew nearer, he could discern the high rock and the curved hull of the longboat looming black against the sky.

He went up the rudder, without waiting for the others.

A sword flashed.

Thor went back on his heels, his shoulders hitting empty air. The axe in his right hand came up, almost of its own volition. Steel met steel, and sparks flared.

Malgrim loomed burly and huge, his beard bristling. The Black Priest chuckled. "What Aava did not do, I will do!" As he spoke, he was bringing his blade around in a mighty, whistling swing.

Thor was rammed against the low shield-wall that dug into the backs of his knees. There was no room to move, no space for footwork. Malgrim's flat blade caught him alongside the head. Thor went over the low shield-wall into roaring blackness.

How long he lay there, helpless, he did not know. But it was the scream tearing from Karola's throat that brought him staggering up against the musty old hull.

There was no time to find the rudder. He seized a trailing, rotted line he had, not seen before and swarmed up it onto the deck.

Malgrim had Karola, afar off on the prow. She must have been the next one to reach the boat, had leaped lithely aboard—and now the Black Priest had her. His blade was high and starting to descend.

Thor groaned. No time! Karola screamed and clutched at Malgrim's gatestone, chained around his neck. Malgrim, sword still poised aloft, roared and beat at her tiny hand.

Then Thor saw the axe. With a sob he snatched it up. Once before, he had thrown a weapon at that monster. Now he hefted lovingly a thing so like the double-bitted axe of the North woods. Remembering, he swung the axe full circle—and threw.

Once again, the sword steadied for its downward slash. And then the axe thudded home in the base of Malgrim's skull—the spike between its blades biting deep. There was the sharp *tiing* of breaking metal. A stricken look burst in the Black Priest's eyeballs as he lurched and staggered. He fell forward, left hand reaching for the gatestone that hung on his chest.

He was blurring even as Thor reached him.

Thor thrust his hand into the coldness and the utter darkness and caught the ruby. He wrenched. There was a queer sliding motion of the Priest's body, and the ruby came free. But the Black Priest was gone.

KAROLA swayed against Thor. They stood tightly together for a moment.

"Jolly nice going," said a voice.

Peter Gordon swung a leg over the shield-wall and came toward him. "We watched from the grass. You can play that axe like a Norse raider. Got his gatestone, eh?"

Thor handed it to him. "This means we split up. You go your way, to the settlements. I go a different route."

"Man, you don't know the way!"

"I'll find it."

Thor went and lifted a rotted plank. The red gatestone still lay in the crotch of the beams, winking at him. He took and put it in his pocket. "Now, if Aava hunts us, one of us will still get through the barriers."

Thor put an arm around Karola's waist and held her against him. He said, "This is a Viking longboat. It is from a past day in the history of my planet."

Peter Gordon murmured, "What queer things this space of Aava has snatched from the universe. I wouldn't be surprised to learn, when all our chips are in, that a great many disappearances on Earth are due to this place.

"Remember the *Cyclops* that went off the face of the ocean in 1920? And do you recall the *Copenhagen?* And, back in 1755, a quay with a lot of people on it just puffed out of existence, disappearing all at once, in Lisbon, Portugal. There have been other disappearances from the Earth. None perhaps as sensational as those I mentioned.

"There's something wrong with this world we're in. It doesn't hew to a lot of natural laws we know."

Thor said, "There are no trees. Just rock and sand."

"Mean anything to you?"

"I'm not sure. There's something tugging and pulling in my mind, but it hasn't caught hold yet. And the weapons we use. Bows and swords and axes. There isn't a modern weapon in the lot."

Gordon grimaced. "Aava and his androids get the loot of the worlds, you know. They grab whatever drops on the planet. If he found guns or worse, he might horde them somewhere. The androids do not have the intelligence to use them. Besides, Aava doesn't trust his androids."

"Yes. Well, we do all right with what we have. But that thought in my mind—I want to follow it up, Karola!"

"Yes, Thor?"

Her violet eyes smiled into his. He kissed the tip of her nose. "You go with Peter and Slag."

"Oh, no, darling. I don't want to leave you. I—"

Thor squeezed her hand. "This is serious business, sweet stuff. I want to find the Discoverer. He has a method of transportation, Peter, that's a dilly. He calls it astral projection."

Gordon looked interested, icy blue eyes lighting. "I've read up on that, you know. It's some sort of yogi business. Certain Eastern fakirs claim to be able to do it. You know, he sits down and pays his brother a visit one hundred and some odd miles away. That sort of stuff.

"I've often thought that mental telepathy was a form of fumbling astral projection. The Duke University experiments proved amazingly accurate. And then there were the Sherman and Wilkins tests."

"I remember those. They worked quite well. I see what you're driving at. You think that the human mind is a sort of sending and receiving set, that it can communicate—"

"Communicate at first, then travel. That would explain your Discoverer."

"If he could teach me to travel that way," Thor mused, "we might really get somewhere against Aava."

Suddenly he bent and kissed Karola, and pushed her toward Gordon. "Take care of her, Peter. You too, Slag. I'll find you, somehow, sometime soon."

He dropped over the side of the longboat and waved an arm at the three black silhouettes that stared down at him. Then he turned and, as nearly as he could judge, went loping across the grasses in the direction in which he had last beheld the Discoverer.

THOR did not find the Discoverer for three days. And then it was the Discoverer who found him.

He came out of sleep one morning, with the mists all around him and the warm rock under him to stare at the great bulk of the sprawling being that lay and watched him. Thor sat and rubbed his eyes. He got to his feet.

"I have been hunting you, Thor Masterson. Astrally, that is. I found you two days ago, but we were far apart."

"And I—I hunted you. I want to learn about Aava. I—"

"I can help you. Sometime after you left me, I began experimenting with my astral projection technique. I learned that, chronologically, I was not hampered in the least by normal bonds. Back on my home planet of Flormaseron, I was not hampered by the bonds of space, but the barriers of Time limited me. I could not go far into the past, nor far into the future. Here, I can do either."

"You can't call that witchcraft," Thor went on. "There is a science to it, but we just don't know the rules of that science. Just as, back in Roman days, atoms existed even if the Romans didn't know of them."

"There are some laws," said the Discoverer. "You have the beginning of them. You can launch your mind from your body and see what occurs elsewhere. Come, Thor. Lie down. I want to show you what happened here in the space of the green flame billions of years ago."

"Will that help me to conquer Aava? I want to visit him now, to learn what he does, what he plans—"

"I do not know whether it will help you conquer him, but it might help you understand him. And understanding is usually a prerequisite to any form of victory."

Thor lay back on the warm rock, moving his head slightly to find a more comfortable pillow on the hollowed rock. His arms he dropped to his sides, relaxing all through his big body. His chest rose and fell more slowly. His legs flattened against the stone. He closed his eyes and lay quiescent.

"Relax still more," whispered the Discoverer. "Sink deep, and deeper still. You must sever all bonds with your flesh. Sink—"

He was going down and around into a bottomless vortex of darkness. He fought to get down into the heart of that fancied whirlpool, down where its own power could drag him free. He fought, and struggled, fiercely.

He reached it. He hung in sunlighted air, looking at his prone body near the slumped mass of the Discoverer.

"Good. You did that all yourself. I think now you may do that without my help. But we waste time. Rise with me!"

An invisible tentacle touched him, flooded him with power. He rose high into the cloudless blue skies of Aava's planet, soaring sunward. Beneath him the red grasslands and gray rock spread out in vast splendor.

Soon now he was high enough to see the great globe that was the planet in all its entirety, slowly revolving. Out in space, in the vast distances between the suns, he floated bodiless. The planet receded, became a dot.

"Now we will go back, far in Time."

"How?"

"Think and will it. Your astral self, your *ka* or twin-soul, is a creature of mind, not matter."

Thor thought, hanging there in black space. And, as he thought, with each bit of energy he threw into his will and into his brain, there was a change.

The suns and the planets were moving. They sped like balls batted across a net by hundreds of players. They slid in ancient grooves, rotating and retreating, going back the paths of their orbits. A ball of raging fire looped at them. Thor paused in instinctive dismay; he sought to turn and flee, dreading the vast sun coming at him.

"Move not. It cannot harm you."

He was in the midst of a roaring red inferno, feeling nothing of its annihilating heat. An instant later it was gone, raging gustily down the tracks of Time.

Thor stared. There were fewer stars now, only a couple of hundred of parsecs away. This universe was retreating away from him.

"We must follow!"

"No need. They will return."

"But an expanding universe means that it will be retreating now, going back to ultimate beginnings—"

"Our universe—the universe of Earth and Flormaseron—is an expanding universe. But here, in Aava's worlds, there is no room for expansion. This is a finite universe, gigantic, but rimmed with some strange force that keeps it separate from our universe.

"Here the suns and planets rotate around each other, but at the same time they revolve inside this space. They traverse this great bubble thousands of times through the ages. Watch. You will see them return."

Thor hung there, in utter blackness. And then, far and faint, in the opposite direction from which the suns had gone, they came. At first they were pinpoints, then dots. They came nearer, great fiery orbs.

He sought to turn and flee.

"Two hundred million years have passed, Thor Masterson. Let us drop down, toward the planet of Aava."

There was only one vast desert of sand facing them, as they hovered above the surface of the slowly revolving planet. Dunes a hundred miles high, whipped with savage and incessant winds. They saw sandstorms that were titanic in their fury.

"Sand," thought Thor. "Mile after mile of silicon dioxide."

"Drop down. Go through the sand."

Grayish granules all around him, bringing the sensation of suffocation until he grew used to it. The gray darkened and grew black as pitch.

"Rock," whispered the Discoverer, "be cautious, now."

They slid from the blackness into the green light. This was a cave, seemingly endless. Embedded into walls and sides, glittering and sparkling, were bits of onyx, carnelian, opal and amethyst. Thor caught his breath at the iridescent wonder of the jeweled cavern.

"Far off, Thor, to the right. Look there."

Brilliant green fire, rising and falling... Alive, and waiting.

"Aava!"

"Careful. Think not so harshly. He will be aware of you. Come. It is time to go."

They went back, high into space.

Once again the planets and the stars left them alone, and again they came. But this time the planet Aava was molten, filled with shooting flames, burning with white, silvery flames.

Thor and the Discoverer went down into the bowels of the planet, seeking Aava. They found the green flame burning with brilliance in a sea of molten rocks. It leaped and danced, and gathered bits of matter around it, as though weaving a garment for itself.

"That is the oval in which we saw him encased," said Thor.

"Pure quartz. When hot, it goes cherry-red."

"This is four hundred million years ago. He is truly eternal."

There was amusement in the Discoverer's mind as he said, "We will go back even further, back to the remotest beginnings. And even then, Aava was."

EIGHT TIMES the universe came to them and receded. At last they stood in utter darkness, for a long time. There were no stars, no suns. There was emptiness.

"We are in the very dawn of all things. We are so far back that there is no Time, no Space. Only emptiness."

"If there is nothing, what are we here for?"

"Wait."

Faint rosy shafts of light streamed up from nothingness, incredible distances away. The light bathed them, sent tingles of electrical power throbbing through their beings. Although he was only brain, Thor felt that force. It was something from beyond, godlike.

Where there had been emptiness, was now matter. Here and there were stars. "Is this creation?"

"Call it creation. Call it a life force coming from somewhere that our animal minds can never fathom. Say the force gathered the floating electrons and bound them into balled suns. And in one of the suns, we will find what we seek."

They hunted through the weird wonders of this weird universe. And deep in the heart of a gigantic star that pulsed and threw its forces hundreds of thousands of miles high, they saw it.

A green blob, restlessly burning, circling within itself, like a fluid always in motion. Cradled and warmed by the heat of the star, given not only existence, but life itself by the rosy shafts of light, was Aava.

"Not eternal. But almost so."

"Master of this cancerous universe, this alien from known Time and known Space. Remember, the only thing that penetrated the force-shell around this space-cancer was the light, the rosy light."

"Aava is not absorbed by the sun."

"He is different."

"And being composed as we are composed would be gone in less than a fraction of a second, in that heat."

The Discoverer whispered, "Is that knowledge any help to you, Thor Masterson?"

"I don't know. The idea in the back of my head, which hammered away at me ever since I met Aava—I almost have it. It is there, if I can find a way to—"

Loneliness!

Hanging in this space, hundreds of millions of years from his body, Thor Masterson was alone.

"Discoverer! Where are you? Speak to me!"

There was empty silence.

Thor wondered. He was not afraid, for fright is a bodily thing, where the heart pumps faster and the skin grows white while the blood is sucked into the belly. This feeling was different.

He knew he was alone, that something had happened to the Discoverer. He called and received no answer.

Can I return? Thor asked himself. Can my mind span the countless eons between my body and my brain? He had learned all he could, out here in the beginnings of things. It was time to go back, now.

He took thought, calmly and dispassionately. There was no panic in him. He was a child with a new toy, turning it and examining it, feeling it bend to pressure, putting it to mouth to know its taste. Slowly he forced his brain into patterns, forming it with mental energy, twisting it into different shape.

Thor had to go forward in Time, swiftly. He must learn what had happened to the Discoverer, quest after Aava. He thought, and in thinking, found a new delight.

How long he hung there in the black voids, he never knew. But up from darkness came a white ball of flame that was Aava's planet, with its sun and attendant moons. They circled in darkness, weird and eerie in their iridescent brilliance.

I have succeeded, he reflected. That is the planet, bubbling with molten rock. Inside that sphere, Aava is fashioning a garment for himself, molding it from crystal quartz. Somewhere on the other side of the universe, the sun that held him spewed him out, with the nucleus for his planet and its moons. I am speeding into the future.

Again and again Aava's planet and its sun and moons returned, to flee across the gulfs of space. Ten times they came and went; the last time, Thor knew he would have to wait no longer.

He dropped toward the planet as it circled its sun. He swept through heaviside and stratosphere. He plummeted into fluffy cloudbanks. Beneath him he could see red grasslands and bare rock. Across one rock was slumped the massive form of the Discoverer.

To one side of the Discoverer lay the body of Thor Masterson. The brain that was part of that body entered it.

There was coldness and a sense of numbness. He could not move a muscle. Thor sent relays of orders along his nerves into every part of his body. A muscle twitched. He opened his eyes.

It took time, returning from such a journey; but at last Thor could move his arms. He rubbed his chest and loins, massaged his legs. Weakly, he stood up.

"Discoverer!"

It was a cry of anguish. The blob of jellied flesh lay seared and burned. Little blisters covered the massy body like globules of sweat. Where the blisters were greatest, the outer mass of the body was broken open into crevices, like the cracks in a human brain.

"Aava did this," whispered Thor. "They brought him in the urn, and he killed the Discoverer. And he spared me. That was a blunder."

It occurred to him that he was granted life because Aava thought he could use him. "He'll see. I'll show him what I can do."

Raging, he brought out the gatestone, staring at it. "You hear me, Aava? I'll get you yet. I'll find a way to beat you. There must be a way. There has to be a way!"

The ruby lay, warmly glowing. Aava was not inside its red crystalline substance! Thor closed his fist on the ruby and shook it back and forth. He culled oaths from lumber camp and battlefield. He swore them all.

He spent himself, there on the red grasslands. Dry-eyed, but grieving, he put out a hand and touched the blistered body. He whispered a farewell under his breath and turned his head to the north.

ALL NIGHT LONG Thor went at an easy lope across the plains. Just as dawn came up with red lances of light across the horizon, he stopped and turned the gatestone.

"If he wants me, he'll have to find me," he said. "I'll lead him a chase that—"

The rest choked off in water. He was in blue depths, in cold clear water that was so transparent he could see a shimmering forest of crimson coral and white sands far below him. Thor swam upward, aided by the natural buoyancy of his big body.

He treaded water a hundred yards from a shore where dead bodies lay scattered like leaves after a windstorm. There two androids lay broken in half; beyond them a fighter clad in reddish fur rotted. The rising sun glinted on a shattered spear in the hands of a Zarathzan, slid on to the blade of a sword buried in an android's skull.

He clambered, dripping, from the sea. Sorrowing, he walked among the bodies, recognizing many beside whom he had fought in the women's compound.

Something groaned, ahead of him. It was Morlon, hairy torso riddled with arrows, his black fur dyed red. Thor knelt and lifted his head to a knee.

"Aava came into the gatestone you gave Peter Gordon, Thor," muttered the dying man. "He saw where we went. We fled as swiftly as we could with the women, but Aava's androids crossed the Undying Sea in ships and caught us."

Thor's lips curled in anger. "Always Aava!"

"We fought a rear-guard fight, all the way. I fell here. I don't know what happened to the others. They went on—"

THE giant Morlon stiffened suddenly, muscles ridging over legs and arms. His eyes rolled backwards.

Thor put him down on the sandy shore, gently.

He went on, along the path made clear by fallen bodies, by dropped weapons. Here was havoc wrought on man and android by sharp steel, by the honed edge of war-arrows and spears. Thor saw that there lay more androids than men.

Toward evening he heard them. Hoarse war cries throbbed in the air. He crawled up over a lip of rock.

Before him lay the settlement, a low-walled city of kiosks and towers, their dun clay surfaces ornamented with ochre and vermilion. On its broad walls were archers and spearmen, patrolling during a lull in the battle. The low tents of the androids penned in the city, ringing it with pointed pennon-poles.

Thor gathered himself. He lifted his axe, swung it loosely to accustom his hand and arm to its feel. There was no way leading between those robot-tents, but Thor knew there was an invisible path leading to the settlement walls, a road he had to cleave with axe and feet.

He stood up, grim and gaunt against the bright sky.

Standing, he could see beyond the lip of rock, away to his right. Androids were tied to chains there, pulling. They were dragging great wagons filled with huge urns. Aava in the urn! He was coming, to blast the walls with his titanic power!

Thor stifled a sob of anger and leaped forward. He ran as runs the deer, barely touching the passing ground with his feet, but flying swiftly. His axe was steady in his hand.

This was his one chance, when they were bringing Aava to the city. The androids would be occupied with their master. They would not be prepared for anyone trying to get in the city.

If anyone noticed him, they paid him no heed. He was almost under the wails when three androids sprang from the shelter of a tent to meet him with naked swords.

Thor never stopped his rush. The axe lifted and swung, went back and swung up again. One android remained standing, coming in swiftly, throwing himself in a desperate lunge.

Thor sidestepped, pecked with the point of the axe right into the middle of the forehead. There was a sharp scream, and then the ponderous gates were opening before him. Thor dove through as spears whistled over his head.

Yorg grinned, slapping Thor on naked shoulder. "We thought you dead. Gordon and Kor Tan will be glad to see you."

"And Karola?"

Yorg laughed. "She pines, the yellow one. But come."

Along clay-brick streets they went, as Thor told of the urns they were bringing from the shore. He scowled and shook his white-furred head. "We cannot last when Aava sears holes in our walls. The androids will come, and then the Outlaws will be no more."

"If we had some wood on this accursed planet," growled Thor, "I might be able to rig a catapult."

He explained the function of the catapult to Yorg, who nodded, lips tightly drawn. In his eyes was the flicker of a new hope. "It might be. We gather what we can from the space wrecks that the planet gathers.

Other things we steal. We have some wood stored. And some cording. I will get to work at once."

Yorg led Thor to a great circular building with walls of glass, where sunlight fused across a tile floor, making the room alive with light. A girl with long yellow hair turned from a group at the end of the chamber. She screamed her delight.

"Thor! Peter, Slag, it's Thor!"

Their delight chased the worry from their eyes and faces for a few moments, as they shook his hand and pounded his shoulders. Peter Gordon said, "Jolly good to have you back, old man. But I'm afraid even having you here won't do any good. The androids have us surrounded. You say they are bringing Aava in the urns. Looks as though it's all over."

"Not yet," Thor growled, and told them of the Discoverer, and the astral voyage they had made.

Gordon wrinkled furrowed brows. "Can't see what good knowing that is, you know. It—"

"Think, man. I'm not too good at chemistry, but there are clues and hints all over this planet. Most of it is sand, rolling mile after mile. Even the red grasslands have sandy beds. And the rocks. There is almost; as much rock as sand. What do you and the robots build your cities of? Clay! What jewels are embedded in the cave where Aava dwells? Opal, onyx, carnelian, jasper!

"Aava lives in a circle of pure quartz. Look!"

THOR put his hand in his pocket, drew out tiny green flecks of crystal. "I got this by scraping the urn where Aava appeared to his androids in the temple. It's glass! Something in Aava's nature was hardened by oxygen, and the sand in the substance of the urn turned into glass!

"When the Discoverer took me out into space and back in Time, when I saw the worlds of this space-realm created, one thing struck me. I watched Aava and his planet evolve from an empty void, saw the planet grow and take form.

"Gordon, I saw no fern forests, no great jungles of vegetation whose rotting and sinking into peat bogs gave us coal. Coal is carbon. And there were no petroleum wells, and petroleum is a compound of hydrocarbons."

Gordon rubbed his chin, frowning. "It's all jolly interesting, old man."

Thor waved a hand. "Can't you see? It all argues just one thing. No coal, no oil. No forms of carbon at all. Just quartz, sand, onyx, jasper, clay, carnelian, opal, rock—all forms of silicon.

"Aava is silicate life, where we are carbon life!"

The Englishman whistled low.

Thor went on, "Silicon is almost as ingenious as carbon. Both have a valence of six. Both unite with other substances to form various compounds. But, just as life with carbon structure cannot stand its own refuse—the carbon dioxide that we exhale when we breathe, so life with a silicate base cannot stand its own refuse—silicon dioxide—or *sand!*"

"Afraid I'm rather stupid, old man. Not following you very well."

"Human beings exhale carbon dioxide when they breathe, after taking the oxygen into their lungs to help release their energy. But if they breathed only that refuse, or carbon dioxide, they would soon die. The same with a being formed of silicon, such as Aava is. He forms sand—silicon dioxide—as his debris when he removes the oxygen from the air that is necessary to his life. Suppose we fed only sand to Aava?"

"You mean it would smother him?"

"You're thinking of human death. This is different. Why must all death be a matter of limp, lifeless clay? Why couldn't silicon beings die and become—"

"Of course. Sand and the heat generated by Aava's flame, plus the high silicate content in the flame itself— *glass!*"

"And glass is a form of death."

Gordon stared at him with wide blue eyes. "Man, man. You've solved it. But how can we get that sand onto Aava without getting killed ourselves? Even supposing we can get out of this trap?"

"You'll have to create a diversion. An attack on the urns. At night. I'll slip out and get to the Undying Sea. I'll swim underwater. I'll need a length of clay pipe to breathe through. And before I go, I want to make one more trip to the Mountains of Distortion. I remember there was a lot of sand over the cave of Aava. I want to check that. If true, one man might kill him. I'm going to try, anyhow."

Thor walked around the room, eyes gleaming brightly. He said, "Peter, we have a world here that we can make our own.

We're locked inside a bubble of space, a cancerous growth that keeps this universe and our old universe apart. We are free to make whatever kind of place we want, in here. It's up to us to do it. We can't fail."

Outside the walls, they heard the deep-throated roar of the androids as the urns rolled forward. Gordon said simply, "If you succeed, it will have to be soon. Or there will be none left to profit by it!"

CHAPTER FOUR

SUNLIGHT GLINTED ON THE flat surface of the Undying Sea. Near its sandy shore, an almost naked man clambered wet and dripping from its waters. In his right hand he carried a giant axe. In his left was a length of clay tubing. He paused and tossed the tube into the water, watched the ripples spread as it hit and sank

Thor Masterson turned his face toward the black hulk of mountain far to the west. Around his loins was wrapped a cloth fitted with strips of toughened leather. Soft skin sandals protected his feet from the bite and burn of hot sands and rocks.

He ran smoothly, easily as the American Indian, at a lope that decimated distance... When sweat beaded his body, he found a pool and lay in its cool waters until fit to go on. Hammering away at him was the remembrance of the Outlaw settlement, of the androids storming the walls, of the urns rolling forward and tilting. Once in a while a stone from Yorg's crude catapults would overturn an urn, but the hits would be scarce.

While the attack went on, he lay on a smooth table and disassociated his astral self from his body. In spirit form he roamed the planet, seeking Aava. Deep in the bowels of the black mountain he had finally found him.

Thor dared not reveal his presence, or Aava would have lashed out with that titanic power that was destructive even to his projected self. Instead, he went down from the thin crust of rock over Aava, sinking through the golden granules of what had once been a great desert, to the fine crust of jewel-embedded rock that was the roof of Aava's cave.

Between jewels, hovering in rock and sand, Thor had looked down on the Green Flame.

Aava was verdant brilliance in the red quartz oval, his inner fires moving fluidly, pulsing, beating. He seemed to slumber, thoughts far away. Thor knew where his thoughts were: at the Outlaw settlement.

Thor looked around him, studying the thin crust of rock, the jewels, the overhanging sands. Beneath the rock crust was a lip of stone bridge, five feet down from the rock roof. Thor had grinned, and slid back up through the sand and stone.

The rock cut into his feet as he climbed. Up sheer cliff sides, using fingers to clutch at stone projections, digging holes with his toes where no holds ought to be dug, hugging stone with his chest and belly, he went. By inch and by foot he climbed.

Night came while he stood on a yard, wide natural path. Thor grunted, eyeing it. Sleep was what he wanted; sleep was what his tired muscles craved. But he went on.

Into the darkness, where a misstep would send him plummeting to jagged rocks thousands of feet below, Thor crept. He crawled, vertically.

Above him he could see green light, faint tendrils of it.

That was the crevice, the entrance to the Cave of Aava.

AND at the Outlaw settlement, Peter Gordon whistled arrows at the heads of the androids surging through the break in the walls that had just been blasted by the urns. But arrows and spears could not stay such as the androids. With sword and axe they hewed their path above the bleeding, dying corpses of the outlaws.

Karola shuddered beside him, handing him arrows. "Will Thor find Aava? Will he be in time to help us?"

"Jove, I hope so. But it looks bad, Karola. Very bad."

The girl grimaced, and closed white fingers on the hilt of a slim dagger. "They'll never take me back. Never."

"Got the bounder...! No, I know. Aava hopes to breed a race of living beings with artificial insemination. But he needs women for that, and so far we've kept him from them—"

Below the balcony where they stood, they saw Slag and Yorg lead a charge with club and sword. The red dwarf howled his oaths as he slammed and battered at android skulls. Yorg, grunting and panting, used his blade like a scalpel.

"They're holding, Karola. The jolly blighters are driving them back."

"No, no. There—another blast by Aava in the urn. Another group!"

The fresh androids drove into Slag and Yorg's flank, wedged in the screaming fighters, threw them back on themselves. A hairy red arm wielded a club like a blackjack. A white-furred arm cut and stabbed with a sword. But the androids came forward. They rolled over the outlaws.

Gordon said sadly, "We'd best fall back, Karola. We can't hold them any longer."

HERE in the cave opening, Thor stood up and moved his axe, testing its heft. Green light danced and flared on the broad blades. Thor grinned wolfishly, and went forward.

Stepping carefully, using the shadows of the stalagmites to hide his giant frame, Thor went deeper into the cave, closer to the green flame that flared in the bowels of the mountain. It was warm here, for Aava was a thing of fire.

On the skin sandals that gave no sound, he stepped forward. He walked in the myriad light that the flame plucked from the gems and spread throughout his cave.

He could see the bridge of rock that lifted its stone arc high to the towering, shadowy roof of the cave. Up there, in the black shadows, he could stand on that bridge and be close to the roof—close enough to swing an axe.

Thor sped silently across the empty space between tumbled rock slabs. He leaped for the bridge and ran up its curving back.

SLAG and Yorg bled from a score of wounds as they fought their fight by the settlement gate with club and sword. Side by side, two against an army, they dug bleeding feet into stone streets, and fought like madmen.

They piled androids in front and to the sides. They made a funereal mountain of wrecked, synthetic bodies.

Slag and Yorg would die here.

They knew it, yet they fought on. The others needed time to get to the circular tower, to fight their last stand against Aava. So the club and the sword stayed swinging, and the pile grew higher.

Now they could hear the trundling of the urn-wagons.

Yorg panted, "They come nearer, Slag."

"It will not be long. You are good fighter, Yorg."

The androids fell away. An urn was coming up. Behind it, androids massed with spears and swords, ready to attack when these madmen were wiped from their path.

Yorg rested on his blade and grinned at Slag. "Thor would attack that urn and tip it. Then the androids would get the force of it. It would kill a lot, facing that army."

Slag grunted and gripped his club.

The urn began to tilt toward the two bloody fighters. Yorg growled in his throat, and the red dwarf and the white ape leaped forward.

They struck the urn with their feet, at its apex. The clay vase shuddered and swung back. A green light reared up, blazing fury and annihilation.

Slag and York fell forward, over the lip of the urn as it dropped toward the androids.

A beam of green blight swept outward, over the massed androids. As a breath blows out the candle flame, so the green fire blew away the androids.

But Slag and York had fallen into that flame, unable to halt their forward impetus. The green flame touched them first, and destroyed them. They were dwarf and ape one moment, nothingness the next.

Watching from a slit in the tower wall, Karola rubbed tears from her wet cheeks with the back of her hand.

FAR beneath him, the floor of the cave was dark and broken. There on the stone bridge, with the jewel-embossed roof so near, Thor was in a different world.

He stood now on the tip of the bridge's arc. The thin crust of roof was within reach of his axe. Thor looked down, full into the red quartz oval where green Aava slumbered, moving and radiating always.

"He's at the settlement. He's blasting away at something," Thor whispered.

He swung the axe in circles. He stood on tiptoes and the muscles of his naked back and thickly thewed arms bunched and bulged. With a sob of fury, Thor drove his axe at the crust of roof.

Sparks glinted. A flake of quartz fell away, dropped to the floor below and bounded. Echoes sprang up, dancing the length of the cave.

Thor attacked the roof with insane fury.

Flakes and chips of roof showered below, all along the cave floor. Thor sobbed with the strain of his eerie battle. His lungs heaved. His arm rose and fell, rose and fell. Sparks grew to myriad thousands as the keen edge of the war-axe bit and dug in the stone.

Over the clatter and clang of steel and stone, rose an ominous thunder. Aava was being awakened from his slumbers. The green of the cave grew brighter, more freshly verdant. The red of the carnelians became purple; the purple of the amethysts, black.

Thor slashed and cut unceasingly.

Like a volcano gathering itself to spew its lava, Aava rumbled. With fire and with fury, he quested for the source of the falling rock.

A tongue of flame leaped up to stand for one long instant beside Thor. He grimaced and drove his axe without stay. The keen biting edges would not last long, now. They were almost done. A streak down the flat side of one axe-blade told him it would give, soon.

And the roof showed no sign of cracking!

THE MEN AND WOMEN in the tower watched the circle of urns gathering around them, tilting upwards. Hugging the walls and shadows of the buildings, the androids watched.

Arrows thudded down onto the androids attending the urns. But when two fell, four leaped from the darkness to take their places.

High in the tower, Peter Gordon fed his arrows to the attackers. The string of his bow was warm. His fingers were blistered, raw with continual friction. But his lips were tight, and his pale blue eyes were icy.

Karola bit her full red lower lip, shaking her long yellow hair from her eyes and wiping those same eyes surreptitiously with the palm when they grew moist.

The urns were facing the tower at last. Gordon dropped his bow, put out a hand, burying his fingers in the smooth flesh of Karola's nude shoulder.

"All over, all over. Jolly good fight while it lasted."

"Thor, Thor," Karola whimpered. In another instant, the urns would thunder out their destructive fury. But the moment lingered into minutes, and still the urns were silent.

A wondering babble broke from the throats of the androids. Some of them bent and stared within the urns, where tiny green flames flickered. Those green flames should have annihilated the last of the outlaw settlement. Yet they did not.

Karola looked at Peter Gordon.

"Do you think— Thor—?"

AAVA knew he was on the rock bridge now. Thor knew that Aava knew, and still he dug and battered his axe upward. He had a depression sculped from the roof. A few more blows and—

The axe dug in. Thor pulled it loose.

He heard Aava, then. A blast of titanic heat, of power unimaginable, came roaring up at him.

Thor leaped outward, away from the bridge.

For a moment he hung a hundred feet above the jagged floor of the cave. In that instant, Aava hurled himself upward, filling the cave with radiance and intolerable heat.

Thor threw wide his arms, closed them on a stalactite dropping its thin rock formation from the roof. His legs straddled the drooping stone, hugging it.

Aava raged, biting and burning at the stone bridge, seeking his quarry. Sullenly, he dropped back within the quartz oval.

Thor almost missed the bridge, leaping back for it. His hands scrabbled at the loose shale, sliding and slipping, before his fingers tightened on a rough projection.

With insane might, he flung himself and his axe again at the depression. Before Aava gathered himself once more, he had to do it.

The axe dug in. When he pulled it loose, a few flecks of sand slid with it. The thin grains showered downward, running in a steady stream.

"Earthling, stop! The sand must not come down on me. Stop and—" The voice of Aava rose to a shrill crescendo, battering at his ears. But Thor worked on. His axe arm lifted. The crack widened. Tons of sand hung above that thin roof, on delicate balances. By opening the roof even so slightly as he had done, he was destroying that balance. An incredible weight of sand was waiting, waiting—

Aava rose in all his might and splendor, to seal the crack.

And the sand fell.

Thor reeled back, battered by thundering deserts.

He hung on what was left of the rock bridge, staring. Up reared in green iridescence, showered by falling tons of sand that formed a tan curtain around him, Aava writhed. His great bulk was twisted into strange convolutions, distorted grotesqueries of liquid movement. A great spray of fire lapped out and upward to seal the gap through which the sand streamed downward. It rose against the falling tons, and was pressed back and down.

Thor huddled in the darkness, cold and numb. He was watching the death of a god, a god that he had killed.

The sand showered down, lapping and laving at the monstrous green tentacle that was Aava as he died.

THE androids stared deep within the bowl of the urns. The green filament was out, dead. They glanced in fright at the stone tower and stared at one another.

"Aava is dead! The Lord Aava is no more!"

Peter Gordon notched an arrow to his bowstring, sent it whizzing down and into the braincase of a robot. The flying arrow was like a signal. Spears and arrows darkened the sky. The androids fell in scores.

For a moment the androids stood undecided. And then, with a yell that sent shivers up the backs of the Outlaws, so vibrant was its grief, they turned and sped from the city, out across the plains, scattering.

"We will hunt them down," smiled Gordon. "There is nothing to fear, now. It is all a matter of time.

"Karola! Karola! The settlement has triumphed!"

She brushed back thick yellow hair from wet violet eyes. She turned and stumbled to the door. Catching herself Karola laughed over her shoulder. "I'm going to Thor. I want to find Thor."

"Good idea. Jolly good idea, at that. We'll all go. In the boats at the Undying Sea. I haven't sailed a boat in years. Say, Thor will need a fleet for his new world, won't he? I think I'd fit perfectly as admiral. Admiral Peter Gordon. Doesn't sound bad at all, does it?"

Gordon discovered he would have to save his breath, to keep up with Karola's long white legs. He grinned and loped on.

THOR came up from his crouch, coughing in the dusty, sand-clogged air. Aava was one solid pillar of far-flung glass, etched and sculped by his own death-agonies into something that looked like windblown moss.

The sand had clogged at the opening in the roof. In one last, despairing lunge, Aava had sealed his nemesis. But it was too late to save him. His very being sucked in all those granules, whipped them around in the fiery core of him and fused them with the silicon and sodium in his body. For one instant, Aava had become a mad factory.

Thor came forward, put out a palm, and placed it against the smooth surface of the tall glass column. The glass was still warm. The bits of ferrous silicate that had given Aava his distinctive coloring were imparting that same warm green to the dead image.

"As though a sculptor had carved him," whispered Thor.

Outside the cave entrance, the sun was shining and a fresh wind was whipping the mountainside.

Seeing the ships crossing the Undying Sea, noting the shaken swords and lances, Thor grew hot with emotion.

A girl with yellow hair dived into the water, climbed dripping onto shore, and set out for him. After her streamed the others, all with new hope, new life in their breasts.

Thor grinned. He ran to meet Karola, arms hungry for her.

THE END

If you've enjoyed this book, you will not want to miss these terrific titles...

ARMCHAIR MYSTERY-CRIME DOUBLE NOVELS, $12.95 each

B-16   **KISS AND KILL** by Richard Deming
       THE DEAD STAND-IN by Frank Kane

B-17   **DANGEROUS LADY** by Octavus Roy Cohen
       ONE HOUR LATE by William O'Farrell

B-18   **LOVE ME AND DIE!** by Day Keene
       YOU'LL GET YOURS by Thomas Wills

B-19   **EVERYBODY'S WATCHING ME** by Mickey Spillane
       A BULLET FOR CINDERELLA by John D. MacDonald

B-20   **WILD OATS** by Harry Whittington
       MAKE WAY FOR MURDER by A. A. Marcus

B-21   **THE ART STUDIO MURDERS** by Edward Ronns
       THE CASE OF JENNIE BRICE by Mary Roberts Rinehart

B-22   **THE LUSTFUL APE** by Bruno Fisher
       KISS THE BABE GOODBYE by Bob McKnight

B-23   **SARATOGA MANTRAP** by Dexter St. Claire
       CLASSIFICATION: HOMICIDE by Jonathan Craig

ARMCHAIR SCI-FI & HORROR DOUBLE NOVELS, $12.95 each

E-5   **THE IDOLS OF WULD** by Milton Lesser
       PLANET OF THE DAMNED by Harry Harrison

E-6   **BETWEEN WORLDS** by Garret Smith
       PLANET OF THE DEAD by Rog Phillips

E-7   **DAUGHTER OF THOR** by Edmond Hamilton
       TALENTS, INCORPORATED by Murray Leinster

E-8   **ALL ABOARD FOR THE MOON** by Harold M. Sherman
       THE METAL EMPEROR by Raymond A. Palmer

E-9   **DEATH HUNT** by Robert Gilbert
       THE BEST MADE PLANS by Everett B. Cole

E-10   **GIANT KILLER** by Dwight V. Swain
       GOLDEN AMAZONS OF VENUS by John Murray Reynolds

ARMCHAIR SCI-FI & HORROR GEMS SERIES, $12.95 each

G-21   **SCIENCE FICTION GEMS, Vol. Eleven**
        Rog Phillips and others

G-22   **HORROR GEMS, Vol. Eleven**
        Thorp McClusky and others